1

Akira Kareno
Illustrations by ue

WORLDEND

WHAT DO YOU
DO AT THE END
OF THE WORLD?

ARE YOU BUSY?
WILL YOU SAVE US?

Chtholly
Nota
Seniorious

"Mm. My dream came true, I made good memories—I don't think I have any regrets."

When I was born?
I remember a little bit.

I was sobbing all alone in a dark forest.

Not just because I was lonely, but for some reason because I was so incredibly sad.
Had my mentors not found me like that, I think I might have cried myself into a puddle... No, I'm partially serious, since our physical makeup is so haphazard.

Now? Now I'm okay. My life isn't easy enough to let me cry about being sad or lonely.
...What's with that gentle look in your eyes?
I hate it when people treat me like a child.

Nephren
Ruq
Insania

"I haven't done anything to warrant your thanks."

Umm…I was staring up blankly at the sky.
That is my oldest memory.
It was a bit windy that day, and there were few clouds in the sky. It almost felt like—like I would be swallowed up by the sky.
Like if I stayed standing still, I would disappear into the wind. Like if that happened, I wouldn't mind. I stood there forever, thinking that.

…That…that this world is breaking.
That everything important was destroyed a long, long time ago. That everything left is worthless.
I don't know why, but that's what I was thinking about just after I was born.

I know.
That must be the same way you feel now.

Ithea
Myse
Valgulious

"Fighting in such a tattered state is just putting your life at risk. It's kind of weird, y' know?"

Sigh.
When I was born?
I know I'm answering your question with another question, but why are you asking me this?

Life starts when you're born.
And our lives are our own.
For us to be born burdened with something from a previous life or whatever would just be unfair to our daily lives here and now.

That's why it would make us happy if you treat us with lots of love, like you always have, Officer.
…Wait, you were supposed to blush there. Not nod with a straight face!

Nygglatho

"It doesn't matter whether it's the present or the ancient past. Any era with delicious food is a good era."

WORLDEND

WHAT DO YOU
DO AT THE END
OF THE WORLD?

ARE YOU BUSY?
WILL YOU SAVE US?

#01

AKIRA KARENO

Illustrations by ue

YEN
ON
NEW YORK

WORLDEND: WHAT DO YOU DO AT THE END OF THE WORLD? ARE YOU BUSY? WILL YOU SAVE US?

AKIRA KARENO

Translation by Jasmine Bernhardt
Cover art by ue

SHUMATSU NANI SHITEMASUKA? ISOGASHIIDESUKA? SUKUTTEMORATTEIIDESUKA? Vol. 1
©2014 Akira Kareno, ue
First published in Japan in 2014 by KADOKAWA CORPORATION, Tokyo.
English translation rights arranged with KADOKAWA CORPORATION, Tokyo through TUTTLE-MORI AGENCY, INC., Tokyo.

English translation © 2018 by Yen Press, LLC

Yen On
1290 Avenue of the Americas
New York, NY 10104

Visit us at yenpress.com ▪ facebook.com/yenpress ▪ twitter.com/yenpress ▪ yenpress.tumblr.com ▪ instagram.com/yenpress

First Yen On Edition: July 2018

Yen On is an imprint of Yen Press, LLC.
The Yen On name and logo are trademarks of Yen Press, LLC.

The publisher is not responsible for websites (or their content) that are not owned by the publisher.

Library of Congress Cataloging-in-Publication Data
Names: Kareno, Akira, author. | ue, illustrator. | Bernhardt, Jasmine, translator.
Title: WorldEnd : what do you do at the end of the world? are you busy? will you save us? / Akira Kareno ; illustration by ue ; translation by Jasmine Bernhardt.
Other titles: WorldEnd. English
Description: First Yen On edition. | New York : Yen On, 2018– | Subtitle translated from Shumatsu Nani Shitemasuka? Isogashiidesuka? Sukuttemoratteiidesuka?
Identifiers: LCCN 2018016690 | ISBN 9781975326876 (v. 1 : pbk.)
Classification: LCC PZ7.1.K364 Wo 2018 | DDC [Fic]—dc23
LC record available at https://lccn.loc.gov/2018016690

ISBNs: 978-1-9753-2687-6 (paperback)
        978-1-9753-2689-0 (ebook)

10 9 8 7 6 5 4 3 2 1

LSC-C

Printed in the United States of America

WorldEnd

WHAT DO YOU DO AT THE END OF THE WORLD?

ARE YOU BUSY? WILL YOU SAVE US?

WORLDEND
WHAT DO YOU
DO AT THE END
OF THE WORLD?

ARE YOU BUSY?
WILL YOU SAVE US?

contents

Before This World Ends——A
-promise/result-

It was the eve of the final battle.

They decided they should at least spend their last night with the people they missed the most.

The legendary band of heroes who had gathered to subdue the Visitor Elq Hrqstn, designated enemy of the Church of Exalted Light, temporarily dissolved for that very reason.

"...So then, why'd you come here to the orphanage of all places?"

For some reason, the "daughter" he'd come to see for the first time in a long while sounded annoyed.

"I told you why. Tomorrow's the last battle. There's no guarantee I'll come home safely. So in order to make sure we have no regrets, everyone decided to spend time with the people we—"

She cut the young man, the "father," off and spat, "*I. Know. That. That's why I'm saying it's weird!*"

They were inside the administrative office of a small public children's orphanage.

The daughter, for some reason, seemed extremely irritated as she ran around the kitchen.

"'The people you care about most' usually means your wife or lover or whatever, logically!"

"Well, I think a few of the others are doing that."

Including the current Legal Brave, the band of heroes had seven members. Two were married, and two had partners... Well, one of them joked that he had "too many lovers to pick just one to visit," so he was an exception in this case.

"Why do you sound like you're talking about someone else...?"

"I am. At the very least, that story doesn't apply to me."

Then a delicious scent wafted over.

The man sniffed the air slightly, and the chatty monster in his stomach growled. Luckily, it didn't seem the daughter had heard because she was concentrating on mixing the pot's contents.

"So you never had a woman like that, Dad?"

Though she referred to him as a father, he was not this girl's real father, of course. It was nothing but a moniker due to the happenstance of being one of the oldest in this orphanage. The head of the orphanage who most would've expected to bear the title was much too old for the nickname.

"I don't have the time for it. Ever since I qualified to be a Quasi Brave, I've been busy every day with training and study, then battle and war."

"Mm."

The reply was disinterested. It was clear she didn't believe him.

Well, there was nothing to be done. It went without saying that the Legal Brave was unbelievably popular as the one chosen by the church to act as humanity's greatest warrior. But the Quasi Braves enjoyed incredible fame as well, even though they were second best in strength and prowess. If they went into any town and revealed their identity, they would be surrounded by squealing fans. Their appearance at parliamentary parties ensured that they would be introduced to daughters of nobility.

But women who were drawn in and got excited about his title and whether or not they were people he could be friendly with in return were two completely different questions. In the end, no matter how any sort of woman called out to him, he'd lived his whole life just letting it wash past him.

Though he was aware he was wasting good opportunities.

"Last time we met, I saw plenty of amazing women around you."

"I don't know who you're talking about, but comrades are comrades."

"I seriously wish you'd just die because you're saying that with a straight face, and it isn't because you're oblivious."

"You're awful sometimes."

"I think that reminds me of a certain someone, don't you think?"

—While they reminisced, dinner was ready.

"Are the little ones asleep already?"

"Of course. What time do you think it is?"

"Then what's that useless master up to?"

The master to whom he referred was the old man who ran the orphanage.

While no one knew what he'd done before this, for some reason he was incredibly skilled with swords. The young man believed the master was the strongest in the world, the greatest swordsman, and the perfect example of how not to behave with regard to literally everything else.

"He said he had something to do in the capital again and went out. Lately, whenever I think he's finally back, he just goes out again. He never sticks around."

"What? So it's always just you and the little ones here?"

"Yeah. What, *now* you're worried?"

"That's...well—"

His daughter chuckled. "I'm just kidding. The guards sometimes come from town to check in on us, and Ted's been coming by a lot lately to help us."

"Wait, hold on a second. I appreciate the guards but not Ted. Kick him out."

"Why are you so serious all of a sudden? Did you really never get along?"

That wasn't it, exactly. But as someone who was called "Dad," he felt he had the right and obligation to get fired up at times like this.

"Okay, food's done. Get your own bowl," his daughter announced, removing her apron.

She brought the entire pot over and placed it on the table.

"Ooh, I can't wait. Man, I've been starving since I set off on the road to come here."

"It's late already, so I just warmed up some leftovers," his daughter said with a little huff, but she was probably just hiding her embarrassment. This orphanage wasn't lucky enough to have an entire pot of stew just sitting around as leftovers.

Well, he would simply pretend not to notice.

"Thanks."

"No need to thank me."

She sat opposite him and delicately rested her chin in her hands.

Real talk.

Even supposing I did have something like a lover at the moment, I would probably still spend this night at the orphanage. I would.

The young man thought this quietly to himself.

Five years ago, when he was still small and decided to take up the sword, it was to protect this place.

Five years ago, he'd swung his sword incessantly even though he had no special talent for it, all so he could return here one day.

Tomorrow, the Braves would face the Visitors, the greatest enemy mankind had ever known. Putting it that way made it sound like an extravagant adventure, but he wouldn't be doing anything new or different.

For something he wanted to protect…

For a place he wanted to return home…

He would swing his sword as he always did—and live.

"But still. Shouldn't you be saying something touching at a time like this, Dad?"

Her chin still in her hands, his daughter complained idly.

"Something touching…like what?"

The father tilted his head as he mashed a large chunk of potato in the stew to bite-size.

"Like, 'When this war is over, let's get married' and stuff."

"...Nah, that'll just jinx it."

When he was a little boy, back when he could only dream about the Legal Brave, he loved reading stories about grand adventures. From what he remembered, promises and phrases resembling what his daughter mentioned were often used to foreshadow the speaker's untimely death.

And of course, he didn't want to die.

So he didn't want to do anything that would set the stage for his demise.

"I know. The little ones are reading that book you left here. I remembered how the story went while I was teaching them how to read and stuff."

"You knew and still said it? Doesn't that make you the one with bad taste...?"

He blew on the stew to cool it, then brought a spoonful to his mouth.

It was good. And nostalgic.

There was almost too much spice in it. Made to suit the tastes of hungry children, this stew wouldn't be found in any fancy store in the capital.

"I know that, too, but I'm not convinced."

His daughter tapped lightly on the table.

"What you and the others are doing tonight, to leave 'no regrets'...isn't that the same as making sure you're ready to die at any time? I don't like that. I mean, what do I know about fighting? But I still think that it's people in a tight spot who aren't ready to die at all who end up surviving. The ones who believe, no matter what, they'll come back alive because they have a reason to go home."

She pouted slightly, then continued.

"In stories, those kinds of people get killed off first because it's more dramatic and exciting for the story... I get that logic, if you want to call it that. It's so sad to see someone you want to live die. But I just hate it when someone dies because of some god's random logic."

When he looked closer, he saw her fingers quivering.

His daughter was strong willed to the point where she never openly showed when she was faltering on the inside.

She would pretend she was unhappy and arm herself with complaints. Even if she didn't do all that, she still wouldn't allow herself to make a peep.

"So you're running off to fight with the gods. You should cling to something more concrete, not some pessimistic jinx. Tell me a reason, a simple reason why you want to come back here. If you don't, I…I don't think I could send you off with a smile tomorrow."

"Ah, now that you mention it…"

He knew what she was trying to say.

He also wanted to understand how she felt.

While that might have been true, he still couldn't talk about plans for marriage. Not only did he need a partner first, he didn't think that was something he could decide by simply going with the flow.

On the other hand, he wasn't convinced saying something like, "*Then I'll think of a good name while I'm away, so get a baby ready for when I return*," would be satisfying. But it would absolutely earn him a good slap.

He searched for another approach.

"…Butter cake."

"What?"

"I'm a big fan of your butter cake. I want a really big one on my next birthday."

"Ugh."

His daughter visibly dropped her shoulders.

"You'll survive and come back for something like that?"

"Is that bad?"

"No, well… It's like you're not taking this seriously enough…" She scratched her cheek. "Well, whatever. It's a deal. Now that you've said it, I'll make you eat so much cake next year, you'll get heartburn."

So you have to come back—she couldn't bring herself to say that much, though.

She had wilted a bit, yet she still smiled for him.

"Yeah, leave it to me."

He gave his word, then returned to devouring the stew.

The night grew late.
The dawn of battle drew near.

†

Not even a year later, humanity perished.

†

Of course, the young Quasi Brave could not keep his promise.

—A long time passed.

In This Twilight World
-broken chronograph-

1. The Black Cat Running and the Gray Girl

The black cat ran.

It was a spectacular dash.

The cat slipped through narrow alleys, leaped over fences, and jumped onto the awnings of street stalls.

This corner was nicknamed Market Medley—originally meant as a dedicated space for an open bazaar held once a month, but constant haphazard extension and reconstruction of the surrounding buildings had eventually rendered it a giant maze.

For someone unfamiliar with the area, just walking through the neighborhood would get them lost, but the feline ran straight through with all its might.

Why was it running? To escape.

From what was it escaping? A hunter.

"Hold! It! Right! Theeeeeeere!"

The girl chasing her prey screamed.

She pushed through the narrow alleys, passed over fences, tumbled from atop the awnings of street stalls (evoking the shopkeepers' ire every time).

Her chilly blue eyes were fixed relentlessly forward, focused on nothing but the black cat's receding tail.

The girl looked plain. She wore a large mouse-gray hat low over her eyes and a coat of the same color. The outfit had likely been selected so as not to stand out, but it wasn't much use when she was yelling at the top of her lungs and running with all her strength.

"I! Told! You! To! Waaait!"

As she ran, her passing kicked up flurries of dust, knocked over empty paint cans, and had her coat flapping wildly in the wind behind her.

An orc grocer, a lizardfolk rug maker, a lycanthrope passerby. So many kinds of people. They all turned wide-eyed to watch the girl as she bolted through the town.

Then the black cat suddenly stopped.

"I got yooouuu!"

Thinking this was her chance, the girl leaped forward.

Perhaps the cat sensed her drawing closer, because in that moment, it turned toward her. Something in its mouth glinted silver.

The girl outstretched both arms and collided with her quarry head-on, finally catching the black cat.

But then she suddenly felt an unnatural sensation of floating.

There was nothing below her.

"Huh?"

Market Medley was intricately tangled together, with no distinction between any directions. It was not odd for a flat road to suddenly arrive at the roof of an apartment complex.

"What?"

She could see the blue sky.

White clouds dotted it here and there.

Still clinging to the black cat, the girl flew through the empty space, nowhere to grab.

Straight below her, she saw Tin Stalls Street, No. 7, West. There were roughly four stories between her and the narrow street below, lined with stalls that mostly dealt in pots and knives.

"Nooo…!"

The girl strained her body.

A faint phosphorescence surrounded her small frame.

Someone with the gift of Sight might have been able to see the venenum inside her trying to burst into flame. They would also have noticed that whatever she was trying to do with that magic would not be ready in time.

Magic was like fire. Not much could be done with small sparks, but large, roaring flames meant it was possible to wield great power—that being said, it took time and energy to stoke a fire that big. Magic wasn't well-suited for something that required quick reaction times.

The girl and the cat began falling.

The light peeled from the girl's body, hanging fruitlessly in the air before quickly disappearing.

There was no time for her to scream. The cobbled streets that had seemed so far below quickly grew larger in her vision. She unconsciously tensed her arms. The black cat cried in distress. She squeezed both eyes shut.

As the ground drew closer—

A girl was falling from the sky.

She seemed around the age of a young teenager. Apparently, she'd taken a plunge from quite high up and had already picked up a lot of speed. At the rate she was going, her drop would end with a crash into the cobbled street, an outcome ill-befitting such a peaceful early afternoon.

That was the scene that filled his mind the moment he absently gazed upward.

His body moved on its own.

He rushed to the spot where she would land and spread his arms wide to catch her. But the body came down with more force than he'd expected, and it wasn't something Willem's weakened arms could support. The result was obvious.

"Gah!!"

In a flash, he broke her fall and was pinned beneath her, croaking like a squished frog.

"…Owww…," he groaned in a voice squeezed from his gut.

A few seconds later, the girl seemed to finally realize what had happened, and she hurriedly jumped off.

"I-I'm sorry!! A-are you hurt?! Are you alive?! Are your insides still inta— Oh."

A single black cat leaped from her flailing arms. She reflexively reached out, but her hands caught nothing but air. As she looked on in shock, the small animal disappeared into the crowd.

"Aaaaaahhhh!!"

Following her outburst, the girl realized how she appeared.

Maybe it had been when she was running at top speed or during her free fall, but the hat she'd been wearing was gone.

Bright cerulean hair hung down below her shoulders.

"*—Hey, look at her.*"

She could hear those whispers coming from somewhere.

Shopkeepers and passersby alike on Tin Stalls Street, No. 7, West stopped in place, putting their business aside to turn their collective focus to the girl's hair and face.

Various races once kin to the Visitors lived on Regule Aire. Naturally, they all sported different appearances. Some had horns, or fangs, or scales, along with a healthy arrangement of diverse animal parts on their faces.

But among them, there were people who didn't have horns, fangs, scales—without any traits that resembled animals at all. Though there were only a few of them, they did exist. Those races without easily identifiable "features" were colloquially called "featureless."

"*Why is she here?*"

"*Tch, that's bad luck for the day.*"

"Oh…"

The featureless were typically treated as outcasts.

This was due to their likeness to the legendary race of the emnetwiht, which was responsible for devastating the surface and forcing all living things into the sky long ago. The most fundamental doctrine in magical thought stated that similar outward resemblance naturally indicated similar characteristics. By this logic, most considered the featureless to be unlucky and impure. While open persecution was uncommon, there wasn't much they could do about their inferior treatment.

Moreover, there was an unfortunate truth that had nothing to do with the girl but nonetheless exacerbated the situation.

The previous mayor of this town had been the very picture of a corrupt politician. It began with bribery, then progressed to cover-ups of coercion and crime, eventually culminating in the assassination of political rivals. Throughout its history as a notoriously corrupt city, a great many people and things had been victimized. In the end, the central parliament had conducted an investigation and exiled the mayor from the island. Following that, everyone had lived happily ever after...but it was there that the fact the disgraced mayor had been an imp became a problem.

Imps were a type of ogre that once upon a time lived in secret among the emnetwiht to entice their victims into depravity, so the imps similarly had no horns or fangs or scales—featureless. Now whenever the towns-people saw one of the featureless, they couldn't help but recall the anger and animosity they bore toward the previous mayor.

It was a terrible thing.

As one might have expected, no one openly persecuted the feature-less. Yet, the thorny gazes that encircled and clung to the young girl could hardly be called pleasant.

"I—I know...I'll be gone soon..."

As though she was being chased out by their stares, the girl stood as she prepared to flee that place.

But she couldn't.

Willem, who was still lying on his back, had wrapped his hand around the girl's wrist.

"Wha...?"

"You're forgetting something."

He pointed to the hand he wasn't gripping. The girl slowly presented her open palm, and he dropped a small brooch into it.

"Oh."

"That little kitty dropped it. Were you after this?"

She nodded twice. "Thank...you."

Hesitating, she cupped both hands around the brooch and took it.

"Are you new around here?"

The girl nodded again.

"...I see. Guess it can't be helped."

Willem stood, removing his cloak and throwing it over the girl without even asking.

With his hood gone, his own identity was revealed to the onlookers.

The prickling gazes and hum of voices fell on Willem this time.

"Wha...?"

No one can see exactly how they look to others. But of course, Willem was quite aware of his own appearance. He knew exactly what was drawing the stares of the assemblage—and the girl staring blankly up at him from under his cloak.

He was a typical young man with messy black hair.

Without horns or fangs or scales.

"Let's go."

He pulled the girl's hand and trod off at a trot. "Wha-wha-wha—?" The girl let out a confused stammer, failing to fully grasp the situation but still following him quickly.

Before long, they were gone.

"...All right. This should be good enough."

They entered a nearby hat shop and purchased the nearest hat. He plopped it down on the girl's head.

It did seem a little big for her, but it suited her much better than he thought. Willem nodded, satisfied, and retrieved his cloak.

"U-um, this is...?"

Having done everything she was told up to that point, the girl questioned him with some hesitation.

"No one will know you're featureless if you wear that."

Featureless people like Willem and the girl were typically shunned but not generally hated or despised, and they weren't treated that way, either.

After all, it was their distinct lack of outward peculiarities that proved what they were. As long as they didn't stand out too much, there wouldn't be much fuss.

"I don't know which floating island you're from, but they don't really like featureless around these parts. Hurry up and finish your business here and go home. The port is thataway." He pointed farther down the road. "I can drag you over there if you're worried about your safety."

"Um, th-that's not exactly it."

Willem was a good height for his age while the girl across from him was small. Plus, the hat he'd just put on her head had a wide brim—in short, he couldn't see her face. It was perfect for a disguise, but they couldn't see each other, which was obstructing their communication at the moment.

"You're...featureless?"

"Yup. Just as you saw."

He nodded slightly under his hood.

"Why is a featureless here in a semifer neighborhood? This island is the harshest place in the whole southwest corner of Regule Aire, you know."

"Home is where you make it. Yeah, there are a lot of inconveniences, but it's not so bad once you get used to it... But if you knew that already, why did you come here, then?"

"That's, um..."

She faltered.

He would have felt like he was pressuring her if she ended up falling silent here. He clicked his tongue softly enough that she wouldn't hear, then said, "This way," and walked off.

But the girl didn't follow.

"What's wrong? I'm gonna leave you behind."

"U-um." Her face still half hidden behind the hat, she spoke with a desperate tone. "Thank you for all you've done. And I'm sorry for causing you so much trouble. And...and I know now's not really right for me to ask for even more, but, um..."

"...Oh." He scratched his head. "Is there somewhere you want to go? Tell me."

The girl's face beamed—or at least, he thought it did. He could only see the bottom half, so it was hard to tell.

The roads around Market Medley were hard to navigate. The streets didn't necessarily lead to the places visible in the distance. It wasn't uncommon for someone to end up lost after making detour after detour.

A tower of junk was the highest point on the island.

Willem and the girl finally arrived there after wandering around, their footsteps clanking loudly on the cheap metal slabs that carpeted the ground. Despite claiming to be a local, Willem's knowledge of the area helped only the tiniest bit.

They asked a public golem for directions, then stumbled upon a supposedly three-way road that actually split into a five-way road. Willem ended up clutching his head in confusion as he pulled back all the curtains in the area only to come across a frogger bathing, then was subsequently chased off by a runaway bull. After racing left and right to avoid it, they somehow ended up falling into the roof of a chicken hut. Their landing broke it, so they apologized to the screaming ballman as they made a quick escape.

"Ah-ha-ha-ha, what a trip!"

The girl spoke more comfortably and familiarly as they ran about the town. It was hard to tell if that was her true personality or if she'd just gotten carried away during the whole experience, but at the very least, she looked more her age now compared to how withdrawn she had been earlier.

Then—

"Woooow."

Her admiration was audible as she leaned over the railings that seemed like they were built only as an afterthought.

It was a good view. From such a high perch, the town that was normally a complete mess when examined up close now seemed more like a minutely detailed pattern. Because they expanded organically and were never particularly planned out, the streets twisted and turned wildly. But looking at them from overhead, the mass almost resembled a real living animal.

Slightly farther in the distance lay the harbor. A portion of the floating island's edge was covered in metal and furnished with everything necessary for airships to come and go, serving as the doorway to the patch of land.

And spreading out beyond it, of course, was a deep blue sky.

They were up in the air.

The world once called the earth was far and, in many ways, out of reach.

Hundreds of massive slabs of stone hovered in the sky, shuffled about aimlessly by the wind. These small bits of earth, called "floating islands," were the extent of the world where "people" could live.

"...Is something wrong?"

The girl peered up at Willem's face.

"No, it's nothing. It's just that the blue of the sky sunk into my eyes or something like that."

He shook his head slightly, and his usual soft smile appeared again.

"What's that supposed to mean?" The girl chuckled, glanced around to make sure there was no one else around, and removed her hat.

"Is this what you wanted to see?"

"Yes. I've seen the islands before from farther up and farther away, but I've never looked down on the town from inside it until now."

She must be from one of the outer islands, he thought after hearing her response.

"I wanted to see this at least once. Mm-hmm. My dream came true, I made good memories—so I don't think I have any regrets left."

That's an ominous thing to say, he thought.

"Thank you for everything today. So many wonderful things happened. And it's all thanks to you."

"That's a bit over the top."

He scratched the back of his head.

To Willem, he felt like he'd just accompanied a strange kitten he'd found on a street corner for a stroll. He just happened to have some free time, so he'd acted on a whim he normally would've ignored. It felt a little uncomfortable to receive sincere thanks for such a minor thing.

"...So is that guy here for you?"

"Huh?"

He motioned behind her with his gaze.

The girl turned around, and a small "ah" escaped her lips. Her expression became clouded with surprise and guilt.

At some point, a lizardfolk with a massive frame had appeared.

This scale-covered race was unique in that individual physique varied greatly from person to person, even more so than in any other race. While most didn't differ much when compared to other races, there were rarer cases of lizardfolk who reached maturity while still the size of what would normally be expected of a small child in other races, while others were born the size of a Goliath, as though it was some sort of joke.

The lizardfolk in front of them was clearly one of the latter.

For some reason, the newcomer wore a military uniform and was giving off waves of pressure despite only standing there.

"—Yes, that's right. The memories I made felt like a dream, but time's up." The girl spun around. "I just have one last thing to ask you before I go. I'd appreciate it if you forgot about me." Then she ran off to stand beside the lizardfolk.

What's up with that?

Willem knew there must be something going on. But she didn't seem like she was particularly pained by the situation (appearances aside). That meant there was no reason for him to say anything. Once its owner turned up, there was no need to walk with the kitten anymore.

The girl nodded her head one last time, then she and the lizardfolk disappeared into the crowd below.

"...She's puny lined up next to that guy," Willem murmured to himself as he watched them leave.

He could hear the clock chimes signal the arrival of evening, echoing from the distant harbor district.

*   *   *

"Guess it's time already."

He had made plans to meet someone around this hour. His assumption was that it would still be a while, but it seemed like he didn't have much of a wait left.

Well, he couldn't stay alone like this forever.

He looked down at the town and the sky spreading out beyond it one more time, then Willem, too, disappeared into the crowd.

†

It has been 526 years since the race of emnetwiht went extinct.

What happened on that land back then?

No accurate records remain. The many chronicles of the time only detail arbitrary "truth," and it's a baffling question as to which relays the actual truth or whether they are all nothing but fantasies by future historians.

However, there are several circumstances that all the chronicles have in common.

As the story goes, the land at the time was very cruel to the emnetwiht race.

There were a great number of them, but the way they mushroomed across the land and flourished may have been the source of their downfall. Many wild monsters threatened them.

Bands of demons and devils enticed them down the path of corruption.

They were constantly clashing with orcs and elves over territorial disputes.

Cursed mutants called ogres were born from the emnetwiht themselves, emerging to attack their neighbors.

In the end, the mighty Visitors even apparently commanded their kin to attack them.

The story continued. The emnetwiht race was certainly not strong.

They possessed neither scales, nor fangs or claws. Not even any wings. They lacked the capacity to wield powerful sorcery, nor could they master intricate wizardry. Even when it came to fertility, they were absolutely no match for the orcs of their time.

And yet, they still controlled almost the entire world.

According to one recording, the two things that played a big role in enhancing their military might were people known as Adventurers, experts in invasion tactics, and the power of the Alliance, which generalized and supported their activities. By dividing classes up, their society streamlined group warfare. By giving labels to the diverse set of talents, they also streamlined the management and growth of Adventurers. As a result, emnetwiht even managed to seal powerful yet scarce magic into talismans and mass-produce them. With the ability to "raise" themselves objectively, Adventurers grew at an unparalleled rate compared to the average, quickly becoming a force to be reckoned with.

According to another account, there were also military powers called Braves among the emnetwiht, which were different from the Adventurers. They were a group of people who could convert the karma and fate within their souls to raw power, displaying magnificent strength that knew practically no bounds. Their only weakness was that only a very small number of chosen people could become Braves, which meant their existence was rare.

Yet another legend spoke of a set of holy weapons called the Carillon that also exhibited great power. It was said that they put ten or so powerful talismans together to create the shape of a sword. In essence, the power stored in each talisman interacted in a complicated manner to transform into a weapon of war that possessed incredible destructive capabilities.

All those stories are absurd.

None are easy to believe.

But it's true that the emnetwiht were the supreme rulers of the land at that time. For that, there was no doubt they needed strength to defeat their few yet powerful enemies. In other words, there were likely one or two truths mixed into those stories.

Five hundred and twenty-seven years ago.

In a castle that stood at the center of emnetwiht territory within the Holy Empire, *they* appeared.

In the end, no one knew what they were. Neither does anyone know what they are now. The many partial chronicles weave whimsical tales as to what they might have been.

Stories of colossal cursed crystals born from emnetwiht spells.

Stories of secret weapons of massacre used by the emnetwiht against the demiraces that went out of control.

Stories of, for one reason or another, the lid on hell opening and everything inside seeping out.

Stories of automated world purifiers awakening, after sleeping in the depths of the abyss since the beginning of time.

The majority were the writers simply putting their fantasies to paper half for their own amusement, with very few actually attempting to reach the truth. At any rate, the world was ending. No matter what the truth happened to be, it would not change the reality that *they* were a threat out of control. Even if the truth was proven to be something like "A single tomato got mixed up in a potato field, couldn't handle the loneliness, and evolved into a being beyond our understanding," what effect would that have had on their daily lives?

But *they* were invaders.

And *they* were mass murderers.

They were irrationalities, having taken the form of seventeen different Beasts.

The Beasts began devouring the world at an alarming rate, and the emnetwiht could do nothing to fight back against this new threat.

In just a few days, two countries disappeared from the map.

At the beginning of the week, five countries, four islands, and two oceans were gone.

And by the start of the following week, there was almost no point in a map anymore.

They say it didn't even take a year after *they* appeared for the emnetwiht race to perish.

Though the emnetwiht were gone, *their* force could not be stopped.

The elves fought to protect the great forests, and they perished.

The underground morians fought to protect the great, sacred mountains, and they perished.

The dragons fought to protect their dignity as the pinnacle of life on earth, and they perished.

Everything began to vanish from the land, like some sort of joke.

Someone finally noticed—there was no longer a future for anyone left on the surface.

If they wanted to live, they had to run far away from the surface, to a place where the Beasts' fangs could not reach.

Since then, a long time has passed, and now—

2. The Unmarked Man

What am I? Willem thought.

The answer was simple: He was an emnetwiht, a race that shouldn't be here, a life that shouldn't exist.

He had a place to return to, but no way to get there—making him an eternal stray.

✝

He repaid thirty-two thousand bradal.

There was one hundred and fifty thousand left on his debt.

The main streets were lively at this time of day when the sun was setting. The lighting crystals affixed here and there throughout town illuminated the area, night or day.

People came and went, swirling around the faint lavender smoke that hung in the air. The boggard touts shouted their promotions. An ailuranthrope shopkeeper was burning tobacco. The young orcs paraded through town, laughing boisterously.

The back streets were quiet compared to all that.

It was silent, smelled of nothing, and lacked the presence of any people—almost unbelievable considering just a single building stood between this place and all the hustle and bustle.

"Haven't seen you in half a year, huh, Glick."

Willem had come to a table by the back wall in a cheap cafeteria. Facing his old friend, he beamed a lifeless smile.

He kept his worn-out coat on but removed his hood, baring his lack of features to the world.

"…"

The man named Glick—fitting every stereotype of a boggard—only gave a small, discontented snort as he counted the money.

The envelope was stuffed with small bradal bills. It would take a while to count them all.

A strange atmosphere had sprung up between them.

"Umm, right. How're Anala and the others?"

"They messed up last month, got gobbled up by Three," Glick replied bluntly, never taking his eyes off the cash. "Gurgula died, too. Remember how Island No. 47 sunk over the summer? Got caught up in the whole collapse, and now I bet there's nothing left but a smudge on the ground."

"…Sorry. That was inconsiderate of me."

The young man dropped his shoulders guiltily.

Glick cackled.

"Don't worry about it; we're all salvagers. When I followed my dreams and went down to the surface for the first time, I was already set to die and let die. And well, I guess you could say they lived a long life. Most salvagers die their first day down on the surface."

He finished counting the money.

"Thirty-two thousand. Got it."

He tapped the edges of the stack of bills on the table to align them.

"...Hey, Willem. You really okay with this?"

"What do you mean?"

"Thirty thousand in six months. You got a hundred and fifty thousand left. If all goes well, you'll be done in two and a half years."

"Oh yeah, that. Sorry, I won't be making any savings if I pay any more than this."

"I'm not asking you to pay more. You should know that already." He stuck the envelope into an old leather bag. "This is a semifer island, and they hate people without horns or scales or beast ears—the featureless. You've got no features as far as anyone can tell, so there's no way you can get good work here. And you're just barely getting by with cheap day labor."

"Well, that's true..." Willem's gaze drifted upward.

Glick narrowed his eyes. "That means this is practically all your savings from these past six months. Right?"

"I take out money for food. The jobs I've been taking recently don't provide meals."

"That's not the problem, sheesh." The boggard impatiently tapped his finger on the table. "Don't you have anything else to do besides pay this debt back? It's been a year and a half since you *woke up*. Haven't you found anything you want to do or a way to have fun?"

"I guess you could say I'm just enjoying life."

"I ain't interested in whatever excuses you have for a boring life," Glick said sharply. "I live for whatever I find fun. It's a sea of treasure down there. Lost tools, material, and technology are everywhere. I love looking for it, finding it, taking it home, and turning it into money. The times I don't find anything and go into the red—well, you could say that's a spice of life, too. That time we made a mess and stumbled into Six's nest, I'd never felt so alive in my entire life—so much happened." There was a far-off look in Glick's eyes for a moment. "We were salvagers. So, Willem, what about you? I know it suits your personality to take things slow and honestly. I don't mind that. But haven't you thought at all about what you're gonna do once you're finished paying this off?"

"…The coffee here's kind of salty."

His attempt to deflect was too obvious.

Glick's face twisted into an odd expression, and Willem, unable to find the words he wanted to say next, just plastered a vague smile on his lips.

An awkward atmosphere settled between them.

The boggards were all fundamentally simple, emotional, and faithful to their instincts. There were individual differences, of course—Glick was surprisingly rational and reasonable, as well as sympathetic, which made people doubt his heritage sometimes.

Willem found that he had a hard time dealing with the boggard's sympathetic side sometimes.

"…Hey, there's a job I think you should take," Glick murmured, broaching the subject. "I know someone, and well—she's got a decent job, and she's looking for people. It's a long commitment where you'll have to deal with featureless, and I hear she's having a hard time finding candidates. You wouldn't mind working with featureless, would you? You are one yourself, after all."

"It shouldn't be a big deal to you, either. You're my good friend, after all."

"I'm a salvager. I left my soul down on the surface. I have no plans to be tied to a job way up here." He chuckled. "The job is, in short, looking after the Winged Guard's secret weapons."

"Military stuff? Secret weapons?"

Those weren't very comforting words.

Regule Aire's military was a public organization, equipped with enough firepower to stand against invasion attempts made by their external enemies, the Seventeen Beasts. Though they had the great benefit of being up in the sky, it did not overcome the massive disadvantage they had when facing the Seventeen Beasts, who'd once destroyed all life on the land. Consequently, they were using every method possible to secure military power, regardless of appearances—or so Willem had heard.

"You know I can't fight anymore."

"I realize. We're talking about the Guard, but it's not like you're gonna be slicing and dicing on the front lines. There's other behind-the-scenes kind of desk work, y'know."

"Like what?" That explanation didn't give him a very good idea what to expect. "Is it the kind of work where you can just follow what your employer tells you to do?"

"Probably not. But well, I'll do something about your documents." Glick cackled. Nothing he had said helped put Willem's mind at ease. "Well, listen. I've heard that it's the Orlandry Alliance that actually manages, maintains, and uses the weapons. According to Regule Aire law, citizens aren't allowed to own weapons above a certain caliber—you know that already. But Orlandry is an important sponsor for the Guard, so they don't want to offend 'em. And they know that even if the Winged Guard just collected those weapons themselves, they couldn't decently manage or maintain any of it with their own technology and funds alone. So—"

"It belongs to the Guard in name but is actually Alliance property?"

"Exactly. Them Guards send out a manager for show, but they don't do anything else. That manager is an empty posting for real members of the Guard. Not only do they have no authority whatsoever on site, they can't be publicly recognized for any military honors since the weapons are kept secret. The job completely cuts them off from earning any promotions for their career. That's how they ended up searching for someone outside the ranks." The boggard's amber-specked eyes were looking straight at Willem.

"Like I said before, I can take care of your position in the Guard. The manager is only a position for show, so you don't need any special skills or qualifications. Just tight lips and endurance. Including the danger pay and hush money, the pay isn't bad at all. Even after you repay all your debt, you'll have plenty left over. Use it to find some kind of life for yourself. I know you have your own stuff going on, but don't waste the life someone handed back to you. Live a real life in this world, will ya? That's all those guys and I wish—"

Glick stopped there, then shook his head.

"Sorry. The number of familiar faces keeps dwindling, so I guess I've been getting more and more insecure."

The young boggard's face twisted into an obviously forced smile, so much so that any other race could tell.

Willem couldn't say no to him after all that.

"I get it. Tell me a little more."

"So you'll take the job?"

"I'll decide after I hear a bit more, so don't tell me anything that will force me to accept just yet."

"All right. First things first…" After a clear smile spread across his face, Glick dropped his gaze to the coffee in his hands and said, "…The coffee here's kind of salty," then grinned.

Glick was a rational and reasonable, as well as sympathetic boggard—a good guy.

Willem had a hard time dealing with that side of him sometimes.

Regule Aire was a cluster of over a hundred floating islands.

Roughly in the center was Island No. 1. The numbers started counting up from there outward in a spiral. Islands on the inside had smaller numbers, and the farther out the island, the greater its number.

There were a couple other things of note. The islands closest to the center—more specifically, those numbered up to forty—actually weren't that far away from one another. Since most of these islands were stabilized by their close contact, there were even places fixed together with giant chains and bridges. Their closeness facilitated a great amount of trade, which directly correlated to the prosperity of the cities on those islands.

On the other hand, the islands at the periphery—numbered seventy and up—were not only incredibly far away from one another, but were themselves not very big. It was rare to see cities, much less a flourishing settlement, so these places didn't even fall on the public commuter airship's circle route.

The island with the facilities in question was No. 68. It was in a weird spot.

The public commuter airship didn't go there directly.

Of course, there were plenty of ways to get there without choosing a specific one. Buying or renting an airship would provide direct access. But if cost was a concern, then that wasn't an option. There was a community of lizardfolk on Island No. 53, the closest stop on the public airship route. There, Willem would find an airship ferryman to take him there.

His calculations of the total cost were correct. Willem arrived safely at Island No. 68.

But his calculations failed spectacularly with regard to a different metric...

When he arrived, the sun had completely set.

A strong wind howled.

"Ha-ha... Man, I messed up."

As he stood in the port district, Willem laughed to himself.

The hem of the coat he wore over the unfamiliar military uniform flapped violently in the wind.

The ferryman he hired promptly tossed him out and immediately returned to Island No. 53. The path of retreat was already cut off.

Before him stood a sign, tattered from exposure to the strong winds.

It said downtown was two thousand marmer to the right. The Orlandry Alliance Warehouse No. 4 was five hundred marmer in the other direction. On either side were red arrows pointing in each direction.

"Is this it?"

The Orlandry Alliance Warehouse No. 4.

Wasn't it supposed to be under the Guard's name, even if just nominally? That's what he thought, but there were probably many things here they weren't too concerned about if they were going to put him in a position of responsibility despite the fact that he wasn't a member of the Guard or anything at all.

The arrow pointed to a narrow path that led into a dark, black forest.

Of course, there weren't any streetlamps or anything sensible like that.

Without any light to guide him, he entered the woods. It didn't make for a very exciting story, but nonetheless, he couldn't sit there and wait for morning. He did briefly entertain the idea of going into town and staying at an inn, but he would have to take the dark roads there anyway. And from what he could tell from the sign, it was far away.

"Oh, well."

He looked up once to the starry sky above, then stepped into the shadows.

It was dark. But of course, he knew that already.

He couldn't see his feet but had been aware of that from the start, too.

Thanks to the starlight that occasionally peeked in through the canopy, he managed to somehow keep to the path. But due to that, his pace was absurdly slow.

He vaguely recalled a fairy tale he had read when he was a child. It was about a boy who pushed deep into a forest on a summer night and never returned. The story went that he was abducted by faeries deep in the forest, then whisked away to their kingdom in another world.

At the time, he'd thought something like that could happen to him, so he'd vowed never to go near the woods at night. Then, his master, his daughter, and the others made fun of him for his fears. But now he could look back on it and laugh, since he was much too old to be called a boy anymore.

"No dangerous animals or anything, I hope…"

That was what he was worried about now.

Island No. 68 was reasonably large. This forest was also quite big. It was fairly impressive, even compared to similar places in Regule Aire, and could almost be said to reflect a piece of nature that once existed on the surface, transplanted into the sky. Therefore, it wasn't impossible that wolves and bears, vicious animals once considered threats on the surface, were skulking around.

Could he get away safely if he came across any of those the way he was now?

Willem considered. For his *old self,* of course it wouldn't have been a problem. His training wasn't so scant that he'd have struggled to survive an encounter with one or two wild animals. Now that he had been rendered powerless, though, in many senses of the word, he couldn't be as optimistic as he'd once been.

Squish. He felt his feet dampen.

He'd been so lost in thought, he'd stepped off the path a bit. He gave a bit of a sniff and could smell the faint scent of water. Judging by the feel and the smell, there was no doubt that this was a swamp.

The smell of water, earth, and wind all mixed together. He felt a vague pang of wistfulness.

Sheesh, are we really in the sky here? As he thought that, a bitter smile no one else could see passed briefly across his face.

Then a light shone in the corner of his eye.

"Oh?"

It rapidly zigzagged as it grew bigger.

Something was coming.

"Is that my welcome party?"

Now that he thought about it, when the ferryman's airship pulled up to the port, a message should have been automatically dispatched to the facility here. If so, then it wouldn't be odd if an engineer or researcher or whatnot noticed it and came out to greet him.

Well, then there was really no need for him to walk all this way.

As he thought about all that, he turned to face the illumination, and—

"Yaaaaaahhhhh!"

The light leaped.

It was a battle cry, one a little too cute to be called a woman's scream.

A wooden sword thrust out at him from the darkness with surprisingly keen swordsmanship.

Why?

He couldn't think of any reason he would be attacked here and now.

This is bad.

It would be easy to just evade this slashing attack. If he did, however, then his attacker, careening at him with full force, would be led by the laws of physics to draw a perfect parabola in the air, then splash into the swamp behind him.

What could he do?

His body moved just before his mind could reach a decision. He took half a step forward, slipping to the side of the wooden sword's arc. He then spread his arms, ready to stop the attacker's tackle with the upper half of his body.

Impact. His assailant was heavier than he'd supposed. The lower half of his body couldn't endure it.

His warrior instincts started working on their own. His consciousness switched gears for combat and tried to activate the venenum in his body. That would stimulate his muscles and speed up his decision-making.

But then bolts of pain shot through his entire body.

He faltered.

Willem fell directly backward—right into the swamp behind him.

The loud *splash* echoed all over.

…The spray of water died down. Heat rapidly began vanishing from his back, which had sunk into the swamp.

There was a small light in his attacker's right hand, probably made from magic. The tiny glow lit up a part of the darkness, cutting out their own little world.

Sure enough, the attacker was straddling Willem's stomach and looking down at him over her nose.

She had bright-lilac hair, like the dawn. Sharp purple eyes.

"Hey! Pannibal! What are you doing?!"

A new magical light grew closer this time, dancing among the trees. It finally pushed away the darkness, and there appeared another girl.

She had sky-blue hair which Willem felt he'd seen somewhere before.

The purple-haired girl lifted her head and said proudly, "I've subdued the intruder," then huffed again.

"There's lots of water on the ground here, so you might slip if you— Huh?"

The face he'd seen the other day looked at him with (most definite) surprise.

"The intruder? What? You...? Why?"

"Hey there..."

He lifted his hand lightly and smiled weakly.

†

Willem couldn't stay soaked forever.

He took a bath.

After scrubbing away the mud, he changed his clothes, fixed his hair, and stood before the mirror.

As always, the man with black hair and black eyes stood before him.

His face gazed back at him lifelessly with the eyes of someone who had never been good at fighting. A vague smile sat naturally on his face, so much so that it almost seemed like his bones were shaped that way.

There was one occasion when he'd tried wearing fake horns and fangs to hide the fact he was featureless, but it was almost sad how poor of a mismatch it was. They were, after all, parts for displaying one's brutishness or wild nature or whatever out in the open, meaning it only suited those who had a certain degree of those qualities.

He checked himself, just to see if the pain was still there. This was what happened when he tried to use even a little magic—*can't believe I've wasted away so much*. A long time ago, he'd been able to fall asleep with enough power for a battle still active in his body, but he knew he wouldn't accomplish anything yearning for things that were long gone.

＊　　＊　　＊

So this should be the facility.

From the inside, though, it didn't seem to be built that way. The floor-boards in the halls were worn, the walls plastered, and several small rooms were evenly spaced throughout. The papers pasted on the wall showed the chore rotation schedule alongside signs like THE TOILET ON THE SECOND FLOOR IS OUT OF ORDER and NO RUNNING IN THE HALL.

Then there were the little girls hiding behind things, peeking out at him as he passed.

"This way."

That girl with the cerulean hair was guiding him.

He studied her more closely this time.

By emnetwiht standards, she looked to be in her midteens or even a little younger. She had no features and was built similarly to an emnetwiht, but…her hair, a fresh blue that reminded him of the clear spring sky, was not something emnetwiht were born with. He didn't think any sort of dye could produce that kind of natural hue, either.

She was oddly calm and acting cold compared to when they'd met at Tin Stalls. But that was probably not her normal disposition. Whenever she grew nervous or hesitated, he clearly saw those ocean-blue eyes of hers waver.

They say a man away from home feels no shame, so maybe that's how she'd felt when he saw her back in town—her embarrassing, unpainted face that she didn't usually show in her day-to-day life.

She's the kind of girl who'll never be honest, he thought. He'd once had a junior colleague like that. A nostalgic feeling crept up on him, and a smile naturally spread across his face.

"Wh-what?"

"Nope, nothing. Take me where we need to go."

She sometimes glanced at him restlessly, as though she was about to say something, but after thinking it over, she would swallow her words and put distance between them. He couldn't come across all familiar with her while she acted like that, so he kept silent and stayed half a pace behind her.

The girl with purple hair called Pannibal—who was probably just around ten years old—looked between the two of them curiously.

"Pardon us."

Willem was taken to and let into a small room with a little table where two chairs sat along with a bookshelf, a bed, and a collection of miscellaneous trinkets.

"What part of this is the warehouse?"

He was getting impatient and couldn't help but mutter it out loud.

"—I knew that would be the response, so I had monitoring and reporting done in form only."

There was a woman in the room.

She didn't have any features, either.

From her appearance, she was about eighteen—same as Willem—or a bit older.

She was tall for a woman, and her eyes were roughly level with Willem's as well.

Pale-red hair poured gently down to her back. Her eyes were a serene spring-green. She wore a bright-green blouse and a white apron dress over it.

Her demeanor was calm yet reserved, suggesting a good upbringing.

The woman beamed happily.

"Welcome to the secret weapons warehouse. Nice to see you again, Willem. Are you getting taller?"

"...Why the hell are you here, Nygglatho?" he groaned, saying the woman's name.

There was a clatter on the other side of the door. He pretended not to hear.

"Why? Well, this is where I work, of course. I was quite surprised when I heard the story from Glick, you know. I didn't imagine that he would be sending you over.

"Oh, and congratulations on the promotion, Second Enchantments Officer Willem Kmetsch. You've advanced with quite the extraordinary speed, shooting so far up the ranks on the very same day you joined the military!"

"Don't tease me. It's only a title just to look good. I have to be a certain rank to apply for this job, since it's a Guard facility, after all... But hold on, when he said, 'I know someone, and she's got a decent job, and she's looking for people,' he meant..."

"Oh, that's probably me."

"Goddammit."

Willem was going to punch Glick next time they met.

I'm not gonna hold back. He set me up for this trap, so he should be ready for at least that much.

"But you must have had quite the trouble in the forest at this time of night. We would have collected you from a nearby island if you'd sent a message."

He was encouraged to sit.

A tea set clattered as it was placed on the table before him, probably prepared while he'd been bathing.

"I've been on Island No. 25 for a while, so I'm not used to the airships. I honestly thought I'd be getting here quicker—I'll send a message out ahead of time in the future."

"Please do... That uniform looks good on you."

"Well, the guy actually wearing it thinks it's too tight and can't breathe."

"Aw, you don't have to sound so sad about it. You look twice as *delicious* as you did when you first woke up."

"So my life is in twice the danger."

"Gosh. Don't be so mean. Just trust me. Didn't I tell you already? Even if I am a troll, and though you are the most delectable, rarest treat in this world, I don't have any plans to eat you right now." Nygglatho placed the palms of her hands together and tilted her head slightly. "Because what a waste that would be. You're the last of your kind. I'm not so boorish that I would destroy that for the sake of a momentary craving."

She looked adorable when she did that.

But a chill ran up and down Willem's spine.

"...Though of course, if the man in question says it's all right, I might think about it."

"Nope. I don't think so."

"Really? You don't think you'll change your mind? Not even an arm—no, a finger?"

Willem couldn't take it. He felt more and more threatened the longer the conversation carried on.

Trolls are a classic, traditional monster. They've been a favorite topic of ghost stories among travelers for a very long time.

Beautiful young men and women mysteriously living alone, isolated from populated regions.

They kindly invite tired travelers into their home, greet them with a feast, enthusiastically taking care of them before gobbling them up in the middle of the night.

Willem thought that was all just a legend or a fable to teach novice travelers not to let their guard down in unknown lands until relatively recently. When he'd learned they were a kind of ogre that had existed since long ago, his jaw had dropped as he stared blankly in surprise.

…And then immediately after, the monster in question had laughed at him and said, "How complicated it would be if *you* treated me like a legend."

There came a clatter from the other side of the door.

There were a number of people creeping about in the hallway. Willem pretended not to notice.

"Tell me about the job. I've been told I don't have to do anything, but I don't know any details. What should I be doing tomorrow? No, is there anything I should be starting today?"

"Hmm… Well, do you plan on staying here?"

"Of course. I came here as the manager of the weapons under the Guard's name. Even if it is just in name only, I can't even keep up appearances if I don't at least stay in the same building."

"The previous manager and the one before that showed up on the first day, then never came back for the remainder of their employment."

"Is that allowed?!"

This job was even more low-key than he'd first heard.

"So, well, if you're serious when you say, 'I'm not staying in a place like this!' then there's no problem if you leave and go live on a different island…"

"You're not gonna say that, then let it end with me stabbed in the back the second I turn around, will you?"

"Oh, how awful. What do you think I am?"

I think you're a demon who eats people.

Willem sighed.

"Well, even if it is a meaningless job, it goes against my principles to just throw it away. I came here with the intention of staying."

"You did? Good!" Nygglatho clapped her hands together by her face and rejoiced. "Then we need to prepare a room for you quickly. Oh, perhaps we should eat dinner first. You must be hungry, right? There might be something left in the dining hall… We'll prepare a feast for you tomorrow, so look forward to that."

Willem gave another deep sigh.

He could never handle Nygglatho very well. Even ignoring how she always directed her appetite toward him (though he couldn't ignore it, really), as an adult male, there were other parts of her behavior that left him uneasy.

"Heh-heh, it's been a year since I took care of things for you. This makes me happy."

Willem was a man, a young person—basically a sad creature—who carried a mercilessness that was hard for his heart and body to bear. Consequently, he couldn't help his heart dancing at a situation in which a young girl (not to mention one of a related race) would be looking after him with such a bright, kind smile.

But he couldn't get the wrong idea. Her friendliness toward him wasn't sexually motivated. It was essentially the same attitude a farmer showed his cows and chickens.

The troll girl was likely showing him such kindness in order to uphold the cycle of "raise with love" and then "eat."

Calm down, my instincts. Come on, logic. This thing in front of me is a predator. My heart is beating faster because of the approaching threat to my life. Don't forget that.

He repeated that to himself several times, somehow managing to bring his heart rate back down to normal.

"What's wrong? You look down."

The young woman in question was oblivious to this young man's struggle.

"...Let me just double-check. You're not planning on eating me, right?"

"Of course not. I really do want to take care of you. But see, trolls have a drive to offer guests the best possible hospitality. I won't ask you to fulfill all my desires (yet), but you won't mind humoring that instinct of mine, will you?"

"Okay, why don't you say what you just whispered to yourself again, out loud so I can hear it?"

"I didn't say anything," she answered calmly, and when Nygglatho rose quietly, the door opened.

There was an avalanche.

Peach, jade, purple, pink. Young girls—all of them around ten years old—with different hair colors all collapsed atop one another on the rug.

"Hey, stop pushing!" yelled the girl at the bottom of her accomplices.

"S-s-s-sorry!" Another bowed her head up and down furiously.

"Hey, Nygglatho. Don't mind us," said one of them...Pannibal, from earlier, with a calm expression.

"Yo, sorry to barge in!" Still another smiled brightly like the sun.

Like a dam gushing forth, they all spoke at the same time.

Nygglatho ignored it, placed her hands on her hips, and stood imposingly before the girls.

"Go back to your rooms."

There was no debating her command. The girls stopped moving.

One of them slowly raised her hand. "Um, we wanted to say hello to the new manager first..."

The other girls nodded in agreement. But...

"Did you not hear me?" Nygglatho peered at the children as she slowly tilted her head.

"But—"

"Listen to what I say…" Nygglatho beamed a brilliant smile like a blooming flower. "…Or I'll eat you."

Her voice was a gentle, like a mother cooing to her baby.

The girls vanished from the room in an instant. It was actually impressive how quickly they left; not a whiff of hesitation.

"Well then, let's go."

Nygglatho whirled around and called out to Willem.

"…Okay."

He answered and, overwhelmed by the situation, slipped out of his chair.

As they ate, Nygglatho kept a bright, happy smile on her face.

Thanks to that, Willem didn't feel very alive.

The manager's room was almost completely empty.

The room itself wasn't that small, but the only things inside were a bed and an empty closet. There was also a wall lamp. That was all. Nothing covered the wooden floorboards. Willem couldn't even find curtains to cover the window or anything sensible like that.

The view outside the window was an inky-black darkness. It was an overwhelming blackness that seemed it might consume him if he just stared at it—or crush him completely.

"Phew."

It's not a bad room, Willem thought.

He had lived in apartments meant for working boggards up until then.

Even ignoring the problems of cleanliness and such, he and boggards differed vastly when it came to their bodies. He had a terrible time sleeping on the beds provided, so every night, he wrapped himself up in a blanket and slept on the floor. Most rooms were heaven compared to that.

He threw his things on the ground and lay on the bed. The mattress was soft, and the sheets smelled faintly of the sun. The tiredness in his body slowly began seeping out of him, and his consciousness faded.

"…But first."

He tore himself away from the bed before he truly fell asleep.

First, he had to take off his stuffy military uniform. He also wanted to stow his few casual clothes in the closet. There didn't seem to be any place to put his belongings, but he didn't have many of those in the first place so would simply leave them in his bag.

It was quiet.

His body, used to the hustle and bustle of Island No. 28, welcomed the comfortable silence. Then—

"What do you think? Is he asleep already?"

"I—I dunno. It's my first time seeing a boy."

"Keep your voice down a little more. The target will hear us."

—the small presences and whispers beyond the door marred the silence. It must have been the kids that Nygglatho had chased away earlier. They could be called tough or not easily discouraged, but they were definitely energetic.

Willem stepped quietly and approached the door. He held his breath, put his hand on the doorknob, and after counting to three, whipped the door open. Again, the girls fell in an avalanche, tumbling into his room.

"Wh-what?!"

"I-I'm sorry, I'm sorry!!"

"Hey, manager. Nice night out, ain't it?"

Willem leaned over, and when his eyes met with theirs, he placed a finger to his lips. After they looked at him with wide eyes, they, too, put their fingers on their lips, as though they understood what he was trying to say.

"Nygglatho's gonna eat us." The shared glances of everyone assembled there whispered the same sentiment.

It was standard practice throughout the world to threaten children into behaving by citing the existence of demons, no matter the era.

He motioned for the girls to enter his room.

There was no time for him to casually consider the lack of chairs. When the girls entered, they cornered Willem.

"Hey, hey, where are you from?! What are you?!"

"Why do you know Nygglatho? The stuff you were talking about sounded really important!"

"Do you have a girlfriend?! What's your type?!"

"Um, what's your favorite kind of food? And what don't you like?"

"Of all the questions we just asked, which are you gonna answer first?"

They showered him with questions, like a forceful rain of arrows.

Willem raised his hand lightly to stop any further interrogation.

"The first question I'm going to answer is yours. I don't have a girlfriend, and my type is kind, dependable older women. My absolute favorite food is any kind of spicy meat dish. There's nothing I don't like—well, that's what I thought for a while, but the other day I saw a lizardfolk's lunch, and yeah, I don't think I'd enjoy that. My relationship with Nygglatho is like a farmer and a runaway sheep. This morning I was on Island No. 28. I'm a lot of races mixed together, so even I'm not really sure what I am." He pointed to each one who'd asked as he doled out his replies.

"Oohhh." Wonder spilled from the girls' mouths. He'd impressed them and displayed a fearless smile.

That was a trick he'd learned dealing with small children at the orphanage. Incidentally, whenever his daughter, whom he'd grown up alongside, saw him acting like that, she would only mutter, "Ew."

—*Man, kids are great.*

Unlike adults, and especially those wicked trolls, children didn't act with ulterior motives in an attempt to deceive him. He didn't have to question what was behind the friendliness or malice they exhibited toward him. What excellent creatures they were.

"My name's Willem. I'll be here for a while."

"You're gonna live here?"

"That's my job."

"Oohhh," the girls once again murmured in wonder. From what he could tell from all the whispering, it sounded like it was incredibly unexpected for someone to come and stay here.

He could see that because this was Island No. 68, just as he had experienced earlier in the day, it was not somewhere was easy to come and go. So when someone was around who typically wasn't, that individual would be treated like an attraction.

As he thought about that, he heard a slightly reproachful voice coming from the open door.

"Hey. What are you guys doing?"

The little ones froze.

It—wasn't Nygglatho. The girl with the sky-blue hair was standing there.

"Didn't Nygglatho tell you that he's tired after traveling such a long way?"

"Um, um, she, um…," said peach.

"My curiosity never dies!" said purple.

"Yeah, that! This is *ear-re-sistable*!" said pink.

There was a chorus of excuses.

"Didn't she?"

"Yeeeessss!!"

Once more, the girls executed a fantastic exit.

He could hear their voices growing more distant down the hall—"Byeee, *Williieeee*, see you tomorroooowww!"

"I swear, they never listen."

She sniffed lightly, as though expressing her stress.

She then noticed his gaze and looked up.

"I'm sorry the little ones are so loud," she said coolly.

"I don't mind. I'm used to dealing with kids… I mean, I was, at least."

"I appreciate you saying that, but don't be too easy on them. They'll carry on like that forever if you leave them be."

"Ha-ha, okay. I'll be more careful," he laughed, and for some reason, the girl gulped.

A short silence fell between them.

He thought she would leave soon after, but she didn't move.

"And…I'm sorry about earlier, too—about Pannibal. She has a lot of energy, but she didn't do that out of spite," she said, as though having just remembered.

"I'm not mad. My bath was nice and hot, so I'm not gonna get sick or anything."

"R-really? Um, then, well…" And again, she fell silent.

She didn't seem able to articulate herself well.

"…Chtholly."

"Hmm?"

"That's…my name. I mean, it feels a little late for that, and it's hard to say after telling you to forget about me, and really I don't care if you did forget, but it's all ended up like this, so I thought I should at least tell you my name…"

"…Okay."

Now that she mentioned it, she was right. They didn't know each other's names.

"I'm Willem. Nice to meet you, Chtholly."

For a second, her breath caught in her throat.

"Then, um, well…" She searched for her words. "…Never mind. Sorry for bothering you. Have a good rest."

She went to take her leave.

The second he saw her turn away, Willem remembered something.

He'd forgotten about it since he'd been so flustered after his unexpected reunion with Nygglatho, but there had been a question hiding in the back of his mind ever since he arrived.

"Hold on a second. I remembered there's something I want to ask."

"Huh?"

Just as the door was about to close, it slowly opened again.

"I came here as manager of the Alliance's weaponry."

"Right." The girl nodded casually.

"And this is the warehouse designated for storing those weapons."

"Right." She nodded again.

"…But no matter how much I look around, this doesn't come off like a warehouse. Where are these supposed weapons?"

He glanced around the room.

He also peered out the window.

No matter how he looked at it, these were normal living quarters. He couldn't see anything exaggerated that resembled a warehouse.

When he'd first heard that these weapons would be used in battle against the Seventeen Beasts, he'd vaguely imagined something like a giant golem, but there probably wasn't anything that big stored around here. Of course, it was possible they were all stuffed in a room or closet somewhere in this dorm-like complex.

But no, even then, another mystery remained.

"And…I don't think I should be asking you personally, but what are all of you? Why are you in a military facility?"

After a few beats of silence, she looked at Willem with expressionless eyes.

"…You came here without knowing even that much?" she muttered, her eyes narrowing. "And you spoke with those children without knowing? Don't tell me you're the kind of person who just goes with the flow without giving any deep thought to anything?"

"Ngh—" It wasn't that he himself wasn't aware. He couldn't find the words to respond.

"Well, whatever. It's not something to hide, so I'll tell you. The answer to your first question is your second question. The answer to your second question is your first."

"Huh?"

It was a puzzling answer.

"What is that supposed to mean?

"You don't need to think too hard about it. It's just as I said. We are the supposed weapons, as you call them."

—*What?*

It took time for the meaning of those words to travel from his ears to his brain.

Chtholly waved her hand slightly.

"—Well then, I'll see you around, Mr. Manager," she said, and this time, she closed the door behind her.

In the Forest in the Sky
-late autumn night's dream-

1. Papier-Mâché Manager

What am I?

A long, long time ago, Willem lived in an orphanage.

He met his master there. His master raised him, taught him everything he needed to live.

His master was also a terrible adult.

Typically, someone in the position of managing an orphanage would act like a parent to the children gathered there, but his master tossed that responsibility away. And so Willem took on the role himself, along with everything that came with being called Dad by those who were children, just like himself.

His master had a terrible drinking habit, and Willem wished he would stop telling ridiculous stories like, "I used to be the Legal Brave, y'know!" with a reddened face at every opportunity. The old man was certainly stronger than other adults, handled the sword better, and was strangely knowledgeable about a lot of things, but the orphans at the time all agreed that *"He's not the type to be a Brave," "He looks like a villain's lackey."*

He was guilty of many, many crimes. So many, they couldn't all be counted. Vulgar whistling at girls in town, reading inappropriate books to small children, not shaving his lazy stubble despite numerous lectures about it, and—

—being absent from home at the most vital moments.

As a result, Willem resolved in his young heart that he would never, ever grow up to be an adult like that.

At any rate, of the many proclamations made by his master, the old man also said:

"Cherish your women. Men can't ever run from them.

"Treasure your children, too. Adults can't ever win against them.

"Steel yourself before young girls. No matter what happens, you and I won't ever be a match for them."

Willem thought he'd been taught something worrisome. He wanted to avoid it if he could.

But even worse, like everything else his master said to him, those words from long ago had become his flesh and blood now.

No thanks to that, he'd been suspected of pedophilia once, but—well, he wanted to forget that incident if he could.

Not having to do anything was much more comfortable than he thought it would be, and also much more painful.

Now that he thought about it, he had been living constantly feeling like time was chasing him down this past year and a half. That was because jobs that accepted featureless workers all had terrible pay, and he took on as many as he could. He worked from the early morning until late at night, sometimes even into the next day. Regardless of day or night, he slept in short bursts whenever he had the time.

And so just sleeping soundly in a soft bed, then waking up bathed in the morning light was indescribably pleasant.

But at the same time—unlike all his time up until the day before, where a list of tasks was always looming over him, his current situation of "just stay here" was trying. In a single moment of idleness, his mind would stumble across things his heart didn't want to remember. It was trying remembering things he didn't want to think about.

Being in the warehouse itself felt a bit odd.

Altogether, there were nearly thirty children here. All of them girls.

Their ages varied, but they were mostly between seven and fifteen.

And without a single exception, they all had brightly colored hair.

The colors were unrealistic, almost like they had leaped out of an abstract painting, but it was almost jarring how natural it seemed. That was probably because they weren't dyed or bleached.

It also seemed like the children weren't used to being around adults or men, so they were very cautious around Willem and didn't show their faces much.

Well, there's not much I can do about that, Willem thought. That's typical behavior for little children, and the ones who cornered him in his room that first day were an exception. A large anomaly had suddenly broken into their small, closed world. Of course not everyone would calmly accept him.

Willem would feel a presence as he walked down the hall and would turn around. There, he would see the back of a small, frightened child, running away at full speed. As that repeated over and over, he started to feel guilty for even strolling around outside his room.

Needless to say, though, there was nothing for him to do locked up in his quarters.

He hadn't brought anything especially like a hobby, and there was no reason for him to temper his body anymore.

He sat on the windowsill and passed the time staring out the window. It seemed like a wonderful thing to do, but there was no way he could spend the next months doing just that.

He changed into casual clothes and took a walk to the town center.

There were hundreds of stone-made buildings lined up along a slight slope. It was a given, but it was a different sort of charm than the decadence of Island No. 28; it was somewhat idyllic.

What surprised him the most was that he walked down the streets without wearing a robe or hood, clearly displaying that he was featureless, but the people who passed by him didn't seem to care at all.

He went into a nearby snack bar for lunch and raised the topic with the shopkeeper.

"Well, that kinda talk won't get you nowhere round here."

The young lycanthrope, chestnut fur on his canine face, answered over his shoulder as he shook a frying pan.

"You'll never stop if you start pointin' your finger at every guy who resembles some ancient baddies. If you wanna be pointin' fingers, you're better off giving a long, hard look at people doin' bad things right now. Well, not much someone can do if they live in a place with too many baddies and too many awful things. I'm sure it's too much for them to count all the things they wanna be pointin' at, so maybe they just picked the historical bad people who stood out above the rest. Then the whole town does it; it becomes tradition. I'd say you're someone who's been through a lot—we take it easy around here."

I see, so that's how it is.

"And since you're an outsider, you might not know, but they live near here. Terrifying featureless, even more than those old emnetwiht. You see 'em smile once, and you'll forget everything about what happened long ago. You'll be too busy thanking your stars you live in this day and age."

...I see, so that's how it is.

As he waited for his food, he sat idly at the table, paying no attention, when a familiar face drew near.

"Oh? It's you..."

There was the girl with the clear sky-blue hair.

"Hey, Chtholly... Um..."

Behind her, there were two girls about her age.

They were the three oldest among all the girls who lived in the warehouse. Well, they were more like midteens trying to grow up as fast as they could.

"Hey, if it isn't the handsome man everyone's been talking about." A girl with faded golden hair rushed over and leaned in close. "And what is this? Greeting only Chtholly by name—when did your relationship get so deep? Can I ask more about you two?"

"Stop."

"Okay, stopping."

The girl immediately pulled back in response to Chtholly's icy tone.

"There's nothing to tease about here. It's just… How do I say this…? We just happened to meet earlier than everybody else, and by coincidence, we had the chance to exchange names. That's all."

"Hmm. If you say so, then, well, I'll leave it at that."

"Please do."

"Okay, leaving it. All right, Second Enchantments Officer Willem, I'd appreciate it if you learned our names while you're at it. I'm the loud one, Ithea, and over there"—she turned around, pointing to the third of their troupe who was sitting at the corner table, pretending like none of this had anything to do with her—"acting like she's going her own way is Nephren. Nice to meet you."

"…That's a creative way of introducing yourselves, huh? I don't have to say my name, do I?"

"Well, we've got the gist of it. You like spicy meat dishes, don't dislike anything in particular but can't stand lizardfolk lunch boxes, like women who are patient and older…right?"

I see those kids spread the information around.

"…Wait a second, Ithea. I haven't heard any of that before."

"Heh-heh-heh. The one who controls information controls the island. Persistent espionage today is delicious food tomorrow!"

"Hey, come on, tell me!"

As they happily chatted between themselves, the two moved back to the third girl—Nephren.

They were a noisy bunch.

"What, you know the girls at the warehouse?"

The canine lycanthrope approached and placed the lunch set on the table. Fried potatoes, vegetable scraps, thick fried bacon, a small bread roll, and soup in a cup.

"Yeah. I started living there yesterday for work."

"Huh, living in the ware…house…uh…"

He knew why he saw the blood drain from the young man's chestnut fur–covered face.

"Eeeehhhhhh?!"

His host pulled back with astonishing speed.

Plastering himself against the wall, his feet and hands floundered for something to hold onto.

"I-I-I'm sorry please don't kill me please don't eat me I have five hungry mothers and an aging grandchild—"

...It was an unexpected response.

But Willem could easily imagine the root of the misunderstanding.

"I'm not a troll."

"There's still money in the register, and I swear my meat is hard and not very— Huh? What did you say?"

He stopped, blinking his bewildered eyes.

"I said, I'm not a troll. I know it's hard to tell featureless apart, but I'm not gonna eat you."

"W-well...but...there's no way you could live under the same roof as that ravenous monster unless you're the same race as her, though."

"—Don't tell me she's eaten people here in town?"

A possibility he didn't want to consider popped into his mind as he watched how frightened the young man got.

If it was true, that would not be good for him. Regule Aire fostered all sorts of different cultures, but they all shared the same laws—a fantastic union.

Those laws dictated it was a felony to kill any intelligent being, regardless of race.

It didn't matter if someone was a troll—rather, especially if they *were* a troll... It was forbidden for them to eat however they pleased.

"No, she hasn't, but..." The young man's ears drooped. "A little while back, a branch from a company of vulgar orcs was here. Blackfur, they were called."

"Nah, don't say any more. I know how that's gonna end."

Those orcs messed with the kids, so Nygglatho went to wherever they were to ruin them. Most likely, it ended with her being seen covered in blood and laughing maniacally.

Willem wasn't surprised. If anything, he could imagine it easily. She was definitely the person to do just that.

Well, either way, Nygglatho was one of his saviors, one of the few people who knew about him, and was currently a coworker in the same facility. He should cover for her.

"Well, Nygglatho's not the kind of person to hurt anything and everything. It is easy to get the wrong idea…er, to get scared because of the way she acts. But underneath it all, she's a normal, considerate girl. If you ignore her short temper and how quickly she strikes out and her low boiling point and how much she wants to eat people, she's nothing to worry about."

Ninety percent of the time, when she smiled and said, "Can I eat you?" it was a joke. A bad one. She probably wasn't saying that because she was actually going to eat him. There was absolutely no reason to worry.

He wasn't going to think about the other 10 percent.

"You're amazing."

For some reason, he was being looked at with admiration.

"Let me call you a Brave."

When he said that, Willem lowered his head as far as it could go.

"Please don't."

†

The strongest warriors or the strongest weapons—whichever it was—they were actually girls.

That was a common story throughout time and space.

Well, of course it was. Women have always been what raises men's morale the fastest.

The vanity of men was an unexpectedly formidable thing. The battlefield was a messy place, where the line was blurred, where soldiers forgot all about victory and glory and prestige—but even those soldiers could not just toss *that* away.

They didn't want to look bad in front of women.

It was that determination that granted amazing strength to even the weakest soldier facing death.

Outstanding armies knew how to use that effect well. So they sometimes mixed women into a battlefield full of dudes.

It worked fine with the supply troops and the rear relief troops, but it was more effective closer to the front lines. Lady knights who ran through the battlefield with superior swordsmanship, peerless female Braves chosen by the Carillon, tragic girl thaumaturgists with enormous power carved into slender bodies.

It was easy to raise the morale of simpleminded men with nothing more than rumors that women were there.

Even unrealistic settings that sounded like they came from some kind of storybook were the perfect flavor for the battlefield, where any sense of reality had long since disappeared.

Willem knew a girl who had been celebrated as a hero like that.

She was strong, but the men around her made her out to be stronger than she actually was.

The girl enjoyed the whole thing, or perhaps it was her only salvation. She would pick up the papers circulating the battlefield, then laugh off the distant tales celebrating all her feats of arms.

You don't need to think too hard about it. It's just as I said.
We are the supposed weapons, as you call them.

But the girls smiling here and now somehow seemed to be of a different breed.

Heroes created for lifting morale had to be a bit more famous, of course. They had to belong to a more popular race, not featureless.

And—well, to put it crudely, they had to be the right age to wholly accept the love of filthy men. The girls here were a little too young to take on such a role.

So something was strange about all this.

He felt as if something wasn't quite adding up between the female weapons he was familiar with and what was going on with these girls.

That being said, well—

Whatever the weapons here turned out to be and whatever the girls were in reality, he felt like it was none of his business. That wasn't his job.

He was just the manager with no responsibilities.

All he needed to do in his position during his tenure was stay out of their way.

…Willem spent almost three days telling himself that.

He thought it would be best to just persevere and put up with it. But he was at his limit.

The children were afraid, and the reason for that was none other than himself. Those two facts combined left him unable to handle it anymore.

"Huh? Oh yes, that's fine…"

"Thanks a bunch."

He asked the girl in charge of food that day if he could borrow a corner in the kitchen.

Eggs, sugar, milk, and cream. Some berries. Chicken bones for making gelatin. After placing all the ingredients that looked useful onto the counter, he flipped through the recipes for easy desserts popular with small children in his head and reconfirmed the process. He started working. He put on his own apron, then lit the crystal stove.

Little spies clustered together and peeked into the kitchen at him—"*What is he gonna do?*" The rule in the house was that absolutely no one else besides the one in charge of food that day was allowed inside the kitchen, so they couldn't do much else but peer at him from afar.

Willem continued working as he felt their stares prickling the back of his neck.

He'd reached one conclusion in his past few days here, and that was that the girls' appetites didn't differ much from Willem's own.

Of course, there were variations in preferences due to their differences in gender and age, but that wasn't much of a problem. The gap between tastes as a consequence of race (and by extension, physiological differences) were much harsher and tragic.

Once before, he'd gone out to eat with a boggard friend (well, it was Glick). That had been a truly terrible day.

Things that Willem thought were delicious, Glick said tasted like crap; things Glick said were amazing, Willem thought tasted like a nightmare.

Though they could have just given up there and then, Glick announced, "We *will* find something we both find delicious," and then the two of them spent a full day traversing beyond that initial nightmarish hellscape. The highlight came at the very end, when they were both gulping down water, tears streaming down their faces, crying, "This shit's *so* good."

Anyway.

He surmised that not only could they sit in the same dining hall while eating the same food, he and the girls didn't have any big differences in taste.

While he was cooking, he called over the little one in charge of the day's meals and had her perform a taste test. The girl stared at the caramel in the spoon like it was a mutated animal she'd found on the side of the road, then finally readied herself, shut her eyes, and put the spoon in her mouth. There was a long moment of silence. Bashfully, she slowly opened her eyes. "...Ho good." The spoon clattered to the floor.

Unable to make a sound out of either joy or fear, several voiceless cries erupted among the spies.

The result was, essentially, a success.

The girls who ordered the "Special Dessert" added temporarily to the corner of the menu made the same determined faces they'd seen earlier when taking their first bites, went stiff for a few seconds, and then their eyes sparkled in the moment that followed.

The whole dining hall was filled with a shining brightness as Willem watched.

"All right!"

This time it was Willem's turn to check on them, peeking into the room, and he pumped his fist in victory. The way to win kids over was with sugar in their stomachs.

"…What are you doing?"

He could hear Nygglatho's annoyed tone behind him.

"That recipe was passed down to me from my master. I hate to say it, but kids are fearsome opponents, and that's a proven fact. That's been my downfall many times in the past."

"No, I'm not talking about that. You won't get any more money even if you take on more responsibilities, you know."

"That's not the problem." He scratched his cheek. "They're clearly scared of me, and it feels wrong just leaving things that way. This is the weapons warehouse, and if they're the weapons, then I'd be a bad manager if I gave my charges unnecessary stress and worsened their condition. So this is… What do you call it…?"

He couldn't find the words. He wasn't confident what he was saying was logically valid, but he said what he thought he should be saying anyway.

"I'm not trying to suck up to them. I'm just trying to pull my negative existence here back up to zero. That falls under regular duties for a desk ornament like me, right?"

"…If you say so, then I suppose that's good enough." Nygglatho's eyes quickly narrowed. "But you're talking rather fast. It sounds like you're making a lot of guilty excuses. You come across so set on fooling yourself that I want to cringe, but if you really are serious, there's nothing for me to say, right?"

She saw right through him.

"I'm sorry don't ask me any more I swear please—"

"When I first met you, I thought you were a cooler, more degenerate, and destructive character."

"That's, well…"

That was just because he aspired to be that way.

He'd decided to assume that character, to live without bothering too much with the world around him.

In reality, he didn't have a very good disposition at the moment, either.

"I'd lost sight of myself. I'll be more careful from now on."

"Hmm. Well, I don't really care. As long as the children are happy, there's nothing else I can ask for. And…"

"And?"

"You smell incredibly delicious. Like sugar."

"I will be absolutely more careful from now on."

He swore that the next time he stood in the kitchen, he would be taking a shower right after, just in case.

2. The Girls in the Warehouse

Moving on—Chtholly Nota Seniorious was a faerie.

This year would be the fifteenth after her birth. She was an adult faerie soldier and the oldest among those in the faerie warehouse. It was confirmed that she was able to activate dug weapons, and so the name of her allotted sword, Seniorious, was added to the end of her name.

Her hair was a light cerulean, and her eyes were slightly darker than that. She didn't like the color herself very much. There were two reasons for that: First, it was very typical faerie hair, and it made her stand out in town; second, since it was such a cool shade, brightly colored clothes didn't look very good on her.

"…Why is that?"

It was daytime in the reading room. Gazing outside from the seat by the windowsill, Chtholly murmured.

She was watching the field in the forest. There, happily chasing a ball, were the youngest faeries and a tall, young man.

Though his build, race, and gender were all different, before she knew it, he'd naturally blended in with them.

It was probably because of that special dessert he'd served in the dining hall the other day. He had made it himself and, with that, lowered all the youngest girls' guards in an instant. By the time Chtholly realized what was happening, they had become completely attached to him.

"What on earth is he?"

When she first met him, she'd thought he seemed…mysterious, kind, with some sort of strange shadow cast over him. He lived in a semifer city even though he was featureless, and he was nice to her the entire time despite all the trouble she'd caused him.

The next time she saw him, Pannibal—one of the youngest—had knocked him over. Now that she thought about it, she'd been sitting on him when they first met, too. For a moment, she wondered if that was a fetish of his, but she quickly shook away the thought. Of course not. No way it was.

And…he was always kind to the children.

Those fussy, pushy, noisy, tiresome, annoying children had even cornered him in his room, and yet without a single sour expression, he'd chatted with them. Whenever she crossed paths with him afterward, he'd treated her the same—

…*The same?*

She caught herself tripping over the words in her mind, and her contemplation came to a halt.

Could it be that we're all the same to him?

Was it possible that those children, little and still growing after barely ten years since their birth, and this Chtholly Nota Seniorious, who had reached maturity and believed herself an adult after fifteen years of living, were being treated identically?

Of course, that wasn't possible—that's what she wanted to believe.

That man—Second Enchantments Officer Willem Kmetsch—probably wasn't much older. Though she'd been confused by his enigmatic presence, he was probably slightly younger than twenty. Then they were, at the most, three or four years apart. That was not an acceptable range for error. She would not be treated like a child.

Or maybe it was because of their difference in height. That would make it a serious problem. This Chtholly Nota Seniorious prided herself on being the tallest among the faeries, but to the towering Willem, they were all very much the same little younglings. There was also the important fact that Nygglatho, who was huge in comparison, was close at hand.

"—Whatcha doin'?"
"Eeeek!!"

Arms suddenly clasped her from behind, and Chtholly let out an odd yelp.
"Ooh, I like that sound."
"H-hey, don't scare me like that!"
"Nya-ha-ha, sorry, sorry. You weren't moving at all, so I had to!"
"That's not a reason, ugh."
She pried away the arms wrapped around her neck.

Ithea Myse Valgulious was a faerie, too.
This year would be the fourteenth since her birth. She was an adult faerie soldier, and she, too, was confirmed compatible with dug weapons. That was why she bore the name Valgulious.
She had peculiar hair the color of ripened wheat. Her irises were the shade of faded wood. She had slightly slanted eyes, a catlike gaze, and a friendly smile.

"He's a popular one, huh? It feels like he's been here for ages. Did you know? I heard he taught the kids the game they're playing with the ball now because it's something a lot of people can play, and even the kids that are bad at sports get a chance to touch the ball."
"Hmm...I see."
"You wanna know more about him, don't you?"
"I dunno..."
Of course she did. Everyone who lived in the faerie house was the same. He was an anomaly, and he stood out wherever he was.

"That's a new hat."

Clatter. Chtholly almost slipped out of her chair.

"You sure are taking good care of it. It's all the way in the back of your closet, and you haven't used it at all."

"Th-that's all there is to it! The only thing those are good for are disguising myself when I leave the island, right? I don't need to hide my face when I'm still on the island! And is that any way to change the subject?!"

She was met with a wide grin.

"What is with that smile?!"

"Oh, it's nothing. I was just thinking about how much I liked your reaction."

"My reaction? Anyone would complain if they were startled like that!"

"Hmm, that's not exactly it, though?" Ithea said suggestively, scratching near her chin.

Then a rolled-up piece of paper sprung up above her head.

"The reading room must remain silent."

There stood Nephren, expressionless as always.

Nephren Ruq Insania was also a faerie, of course.

This year would be the thirteenth after her birth. She had reached maturity that summer and had just recently been confirmed compatible with dug weapons.

She had dullish gray hair and eyes the color of charcoal. She was so short that she would be buried standing in a crowd of the little ones. She constantly wore a blank expression, and Chtholly, at least, had never seen her smile or scowl.

After a quick glance around, she couldn't see any other faeries in the reading room. Everyone was gathered around the windowsill.

"S-sorry..."

Chtholly earnestly bowed her head, and the newcomer sat in the empty seat beside her.

"So what sort of person is he?"

Nephren started with a question. Chtholly's shoulders dropped in disappointment.

"Didn't you just tell me to stop talking?"

"I think it's fine as long as you're not yelling."

"And so our conversation continues... You think he's interesting, too, Ren?"

"Not really." Nephren's eyes flitted outside the window. "I only think he's a strange person."

So she looks at him the same way, too.

Chtholly was glad knowing that she wasn't the only one.

Someone who was *just* kind or *just* cheerful wouldn't bother her so much.

He acted so friendly, but it felt like there was a barrier somewhere.

He seemed like he was having so much fun, but they got the sense that he was somehow sad.

At first glance, he was fitting in well, but...

At the oddest moments, he would gaze off, a distant look in his eyes, as though reliving memories of a place far away.

So they couldn't help but pay attention to him. They wanted to know.

"...How many days left, Chtholly?" Ithea asked as she was spacing out.

She understood exactly what her friend meant because of how the question was phrased. Chtholly was counting down every single day on the calendar in her room, so she knew the number she had to respond with.

"Mm, a little more than ten days."

"Aww, that's plenty of time but not enough at all."

"What are you talking about?"

"I'm talking about you enjoying your youth to the fullest, of course."

Thunk.

Her head slammed on the table.

"Chtholly. The reading room must remain silent."

"S-sorry... Wait, no I'm not! What on *earth* are you talking about, Ithea?!"

"Nya-ha-ha-ha, don't get so bashful! You're a winner just by falling in love, especially in this world where so many faeries pass before adolescence. Aren't you glad you were born a girl?"

"Th-that's not how I was looking at him—"

"I see…I shall go find several volumes on heterogamy for your reference."

"Ren?! Wait, I really don't need those!"

"Chtholly, the reading room must remain silent."

"Who's the one yelling here?!"

Outside, the ball flew high, drawing a big arc in the azure sky.

"…I really don't, so please stop. I've finally managed to give so many things up, so I don't want to make new regrets now."

Chtholly spoke quietly.

"Okay."

Ithea gave a sad smile, and without another word, she gazed out the window.

"…Mm."

Nephren nodded slightly, and she, too, remained silent, opening the book in her hands.

Another week passed.

Of course, it was about time Willem started thinking something was off.

What had he signed up for? He was a weapons manager in name only. It was a military thing, a political thing. A world of metal and rust, of gunpowder and smoke. Well, he hadn't thought he'd be close to any battlefields when he'd heard the position was only nominal, but he'd been under the passing impression that it was a vector that at least pointed in that direction.

Now that he was involved, how would everything turn out?

Tap, tap, tap, tap came the energetic sound of someone running down the hall.

"Willieeee!"

A beautiful dropkick with both feet pierced Willem straight in the back from a proper running start.

"Oof?!"

The attack had graceful form that blew away all differences in build and weight. The moment he lurched forward, short arms and legs skillfully attacked his joints.

"All right, got 'im!"

"Ahh no, no, that's not right! That's not what I meant when I said to get him!"

"All's well that ends well."

"Yep, no problem as long as he can't get away."

"It didn't end well! Because we're the ones supposed to be asking for a favor!"

"It is a basic military strategy to display your strength before asking for favors."

"But that's something only bloodthirsty people do!"

"Blooodthirstyyyy! Blooodthirstyyyy!"

"That's not something you repeat like a song!!"

"...Oh..."

Willem somewhat managed to grasp the situation as his joints were squeezed, almost comfortably.

It was the energetic little animals known as children.

"What, did you guys come to ask me something?"

"Yeah, yeah, we did!"

"We're going to read a book, so you have to come!"

"Th-th-that's why you don't attack the joints when asking for something!"

You're right. I thoroughly support what you said, so please tell them again.

"...You want me to read you a difficult book? I hate to say it, but I'm not very good at reading and writing."

"Huh? But aren't you an officer? Shouldn't you be smart?"

"Yeah, super-smart. I can read you stacks of ancient texts from five hundred years ago."

"Ah-ha-ha-ha. What?"

They tugged on his sleeve as they laughed.

"We can read ourselves. We just want you to stay close by."

"Y-yes, it's an old story, so we're scared to read on our own."

"I'm not that scared, but these kids really want you nearby."

"H-hey, that's not fair!"

As always, as words spilled from their mouths, together they pulled him somewhere.

"An old story?"

"An emnetwiht story!"

An emnetwiht story.

He felt slightly dizzy.

Intense déjà vu. His memories began replaying automatically.

His view of the warehouse on Island No. 68 wavered and was replaced with the old orphanage.

This was where he used to live.

It was a memory of when he'd looked after the youngest children as the eldest of those raised there.

"Willieee!"

"Geez, Dad, again?"

"Ha-ha-ha, that's evidence you're healthy!"

The floodgates cracked open. All the dear voices he'd tried so hard not to recall echoed in his head, one after the other.

He'd forgotten what was important. Why had he stayed so long on dingy Island No. 28? It was uncomfortable. A terrible place to live. No one accepted him as someone who was clearly scarred as a featureless. It wasn't home.

That was fine.

That's why he stayed.

Willem no longer had anywhere to go. Even if he wished to return somewhere, it would never be possible. Island No. 28 had reminded him of that as long as he stayed. He couldn't forget it.

But here—

It was too much like that dear, old place.

—*No*, he told himself.

This was not his home.

Just look at the clothes you're wearing. A black military uniform that didn't suit him. An exaggerated rank plastered on as a pretense.

He only needed to work here a few months.

So he was all right. He hadn't forgotten or betrayed that place.

He'd wavered for a moment.

"Willem?"

Someone called to him.

"—I'm fine. I just didn't get much sleep last night. Anyway, what's up with emnetwiht?"

"Oh yeah. I heard that people like that lived on the surface a long time ago!"

The girls tried their best to explain with their awkward grasp of language.

According to a picture book they read once, the land was full of scary creatures called emnetwiht.

They were scary because, thanks to them, orcs at the time were all trapped in desolate areas, elves had their forests burned, lizardfolk were cornered in the water, lycanthropes' peace was shattered, and even dragons had their treasure stolen. And to top it all off, they even thrust aside the punishment delivered by the new Visitors, who were born to cast judgment, and easily struck down the gods one after another.

In the end, the emnetwiht called on the Seventeen Beasts from somewhere and brought about their own destruction. When that happened, they became even more wicked because they got everything on land mixed up with their problems.

"Isn't it scary?"

Well, sure, when they put it like that, it was definitely scary. What villainous invaders they were.

"It was a picture book, so some of those things might not be true, you know."

"But it said that it actually happened."

"That's what all made-up stories say."

The girls looked at one another.

"Then, does that mean the Braves in the story were fake, too?" the purple-haired girl murmured.

"What? Oh no…" The rest of the girls were visibly troubled.

"Well, some parts might be true in there somewhere… But you're most worried about the Braves being false?"

"Because…" The girls exchanged glances again. "We're Braves, too, right?"

What?

He didn't understand. They called the emnetwiht scary, so why did they liken themselves to something that could be called the very symbol of that threat?

Well, sure—to them at the time, the Braves were kind of like a weapon. These girls called themselves weapons, so it wouldn't be unusual if they felt a sense of affinity for them.

That was how he intended to swallow the feeling that something was out of place.

"By the way…Mr. Willem?"

One of them interjected timidly.

"Are you sure that doesn't hurt…?"

He finally realized that he'd been massaging his joint this entire time.

3. Faerie Warehouse

Chtholly didn't like her very much.

But that probably wasn't true the other way around.

She'd said that she thought of Chtholly as a little sister and treated her that way.

Of course, faeries didn't have big sisters or little sisters, since they weren't born from a mother's womb. Quite frankly, it was annoying how she acted so familiar, simply on the ridiculous basis that they'd been born in the same forest on the same island, though five years earlier.

She was apparently very proficient with her dug weapon, and that was one point that Chtholly definitely wasn't thrilled about. She would fly into the battlefield, large sword in hand. Afterward, she would gallantly return, a grin on her face. Barging into the dining hall, she would wolf down the butter cake laid out for dinner and, with an expression of supreme bliss on her face, declare "I really feel like I've come home when I eat this."

This happened every time she went out on a mission, and Chtholly, who was still young and didn't know the battlefield, thought it was all to spite her.

"...Hey."

When had that been?

Acting on a whim, Chtholly had once called out to her.

"You're always wearing that brooch, but it doesn't look very good on you. You know that."

"Ah-ha-ha-ha, you really just say what's on your mind. Your big sis is gonna cry."

"My big sis?"

"What? I mean, there's no way I can be the little sister!"

"I am not asking you to change our relationship."

After their typical banter, her smile had suddenly wavered.

"I had someone like a big sister a long time ago. I took it from her."

"...Took it? Not got it?"

"It was her treasure. She always made sure to wear it on her. I asked her so many times to give it to me, but, eh, she never listened."

What a demonic deed, stealing something so precious...

She ignored her little sister's astonished gaze with a smile as she always did.

"The more she refused me, the more fun I started having. I challenged her to all kinds of competitions, and if I won, it would be my prize. Our grades in the *training courses, eating competitions, card games. But I could never beat her. I could never win, so I kept challenging her. I had so much fun.*"

Chtholly could guess how it would end after hearing that much.

Chtholly hadn't known the faerie who could have been this self-proclaimed "big sister's" big sister. She didn't know her, which meant she was already gone by the time Chtholly arrived.

Maybe she shouldn't have asked about it. That thought must have been visible on her face, as the other faerie patted Chtholly's back.

"*Well, in the end, I won by default. It's not a very satisfying story. For some reason, that was the only day she didn't wear it to the battlefield. She left it on her desk in her room. So I snatched it up.*" She laughed out loud, like there was some sort of funny element to the story. "*I know it doesn't look good on me, but I feel like I have to keep wearing it. I can't go anywhere without it.*"

Chtholly would say it again: She didn't like her very much.

But—when she thought back on it—she didn't hate her that much.

That was why. The day she didn't return from the battlefield, Chtholly visited her room.

The door was unlocked. She flung it open to find it messy inside. Underwear strewn about, a card game was still dealt... Everything was all over the place.

Among it all, only the desk was clean.

Not a speck of dust lay on its sparkling surface, and sitting there, left behind, was a single silver brooch.

Willem hadn't seen some of the faeries for a few days.

Chtholly, and Ithea, and Nephren. The oldest girls in the faerie warehouse had all disappeared somewhere together.

He assumed there was some sort of reason for it and put it out of his mind.

Not thinking about it anymore, he simply accepted it for what it was.

*   *   *

It rained in the morning that day, and the ground softened.

It was just after the red team, who'd been cornered the entire first half of the match, finally earned the right to attack. Everyone on their team was in high spirits, going wild about smashing the ball into the white team leader.

Then, just as they hit the ball high in the sky, there came a strong wind.

The wind blew the ball into a deep thicket.

The only girl still chasing it hated giving up. She was the kind who paid no attention to where she was stepping when she looked up. Accounting for all these facts, there was only one way this could end. The girl's feet slipped beautifully, and she plunged headfirst into the thicket.

"Hey!!"

Willem wouldn't be surprised if she ended up with serious injuries— that's how bad the situation was.

"Ow, ow, ow…I messed up, I messed up."

So when she stood, smiling, speaking lightly, he was momentarily relieved.

Then, in the next moment, he shuddered. There were deep lacerations on her left thigh. Tiny branches had pierced her right upper arm as well. If he was judging by how much she was bleeding, her heart rate didn't appear to have quickened—the only silver lining in a bad situation. At the very least, her injuries weren't so negligible that they could just leave it at "I messed up."

Willem quickly checked over her wounds.

"They're pretty deep. I'll treat them right away."

"Aww, *I'm fine though*." Her tone was indifferent.

Did I hear that right?

"But come on, let's keep going! We're gonna make a comeback!"

Could it be her injuries weren't as deep as they looked? His eyes inadvertently dropped down to the open wounds—but no matter how many times he looked, there was no doubt they were severe enough that if not treated quickly, they might endanger her life.

"They…don't hurt?"

"They do. But we were in a really good spot!"

A bright, wide smile, full of joy.

He could see faint beads of greasy sweat forming on her forehead.

He finally grasped what was going on. Just as she said, it wasn't like she didn't feel any pain. This girl—and the children around her who didn't find anything unnatural about what she was saying—simply didn't think being injured was a big deal.

He felt a chill.

It felt like he was surrounded by alien, enigmatic creatures. Or perhaps, it wasn't a trick of his mind but something he simply hadn't noticed until now—

"The match is canceled."

Willem made his announcement one-sidedly and scooped up the girl.

"Awwww," came cries of disappointment.

"…So why is it the girl herself isn't upset but her escort is?"

Nygglatho, wearing a lab coat over her normal clothes, asked in a quiet murmur.

After they finished dressing the wounds, the girl, her arms and legs wrapped up in bandages, sat on the bed, muttering complaints about the game being canceled.

Willem sat on a chair, his head in his hands, and without moving, he questioned Nygglatho, who probably knew something.

"I hadn't noticed it until today, but they're completely indifferent about their lives, aren't they?"

"They are. They certainly have that tendency."

"That's not normal. What are they anyway?"

"Hmm." Nygglatho hummed, as though planning something, then asked in return, "Do you really want to know?"

Willem looked up.

"Though it is only a title, you are still the manager here. If you request information, I am in no position to deny your request." She spoke with a vague tone, almost like she was having fun yet dead serious. "To be honest, I don't want to tell you. When you hear this, you will treat the girls differently. I don't think you'd be able to keep your relationship with them as it is now. I thought your attempt to play a nice older brother these past few days was pretty gross at first, but all in all, I'm grateful. I want things to stay as they are now for a little while longer, if possible."

"…Tell me."

"Oh, well. Very well."

Nygglatho shrugged.

"Strictly speaking, those children are not alive. And since they're not alive, their bodies have no fear of death. Their inner feelings are different, but they're dragged along by their bodily senses when they're still young, so it's easy for them to grow careless."

"…I'm sorry. I have no idea what you're saying."

They're not alive? This must be some kind of joke.

But they lived out their days so stubbornly, so brightly, so loudly.

"Sure. I didn't want to believe this logic at first, either," Nygglatho said in a small voice, then she left the room and motioned for him to follow. "Come. Let me show you something."

Willem arduously pulled himself up and followed her out of the room.

"You of course know about the emnetwiht, right?" Nygglatho asked as they walked down the hall.

"…As much as anyone else."

"You don't have to sound so modest about it." She chuckled. "The legendary race that ruled over all the land over five hundred years ago. They were not blessed with any abilities whatsoever."

Essentially:

They didn't have enormous bodies like the giganto.

They didn't have elaborate sorcery like the elves.

They didn't have sophisticated engineering like the morian.

They didn't have explosive fertility like the orcs.

And of course, they didn't have overwhelming power like the dragons.

All their abilities were half-baked, and they were generally considered lesser beings. And yet, they made enemies of almost every other race and were the supreme rulers of the land for a long time.

"...Yeah. I heard they were that kind of people."

"Let me add one thing. It has been passed down through my people that they tasted the most delicious out of all the races, by a long shot."

That legend should just die out.

"One of the cornerstones of their strength was the codified techniques that we now refer to as dug weapons and the physical manifestation of that system as actual armaments for use on the battlefield."

"...I've heard of them. Anala talked about them once. I think it was something like if you could find just one living dug weapon, it could earn more than enough to cover an entire salvage harvest in terms of pay..."

"Right, that's how much the Alliance values them. I think, two hundred bradal at the very minimum, and I believe eight million was the most ever paid?"

Eight million.

It could pay off the rest of Willem's debt (which was by no means a small amount) fifty times over and still have some left over.

"And so all the dug weapons the Alliance has collected—"

Nygglatho stopped before a door.

It was large and stout.

Fashioned of solid metal, it had rivets all around the edge, a lock in a fivefold style, and the knob was a heavy-looking handle.

It was almost unusual how this door alone seemed to exude the feeling of a military facility in this warehouse brimming with daily life.

"—are stored in here."

Nygglatho unlocked the door with a practiced hand and pushed it open.

Fwooooom—

A deep sound resonated in the pit of his stomach.

A wet scent of mold and dust tickled his nose.

It's almost like a tomb.

The room resembled the kind of crypt a royal family would have been enshrined in thousands of years ago, their valuables entombed with them as burial goods, but where an idiot, lured by the promise of riches, tries to steal things and winds up cursed. Willem had never seen the real thing with his own eyes, but he'd heard many funny stories of the sort. Well, he didn't know if there were any left on the surface as it was now.

There was no light in the room. While he knew something lay beyond the dim darkness, there was no way to tell what it was.

"Sure is secure," he murmured absently.

"This place does contain dangerous materials, after all," came the response from beside him. "Ancient super-weapons the methods to create, repair, or even handle have all been lost to time. Long ago, a powerless race made these to stand up to the threats of the giant dragons, the Visitors. A symbol of their will to resist, the power to stand as a challenge. Even though they were meant as personal weapons, they could singlehandedly turn the tide of battles. In the long history of this world, these can be considered the upper echelon, the most reliable of trump cards against an opponent of overwhelming power—"

Willem's eyes slowly grew accustomed to the darkness.

He could now faintly see what was in the warehouse.

"Ha-ha," he laughed quietly.

Leaning against one wall were ten or so swordlike objects.

At the very least, they were swords judging by their outward appearance.

Many of them were much bigger than typical longswords used in ceremonies and combat. They varied in length, but most were about as tall as a person or slightly shorter. Their hilts were long, too, and were clearly meant to be wielded with two hands.

The most peculiar trait was the structure of the blades.

He picked one and approached it to get a better look. On the face of the blade, he could see something that looked like a crack running along it. When he looked even closer, he could tell the blade on either side of the crack was different in color.

Swords were usually hammered or carved out of a single ingot. But this was different. Several steel billets the size of his clenched fist had been pieced together to create the shape of a sword, like a completed jigsaw puzzle.

"A Carillon…"

"I've heard they were once called that long ago, yes?" Nygglatho shrugged.

When he looked around the room again, a clenching pain gripped his chest.

He recognized some of these swords.

But of course, he recognized the mass-produced Carillon, the Percival series. When he had just become a Quasi Brave and didn't have a specialty sword, it had fought alongside him on countless occasions. Though it wasn't equipped with any particular talents, its high basic specs and expandability—not to mention its standardized build—meant it was possible to perform emergency maintenance even in the middle of the battlefield. In short, it was incredibly easy to use. Its successor, the Dindrane series, didn't suit Willem too well but, more stable than its predecessor, had been popular with other Quasi Braves.

Deep inside, there was Locus Solus. It was the name of the giant, beloved sword that had fought alongside a Quasi Brave against the purple dragon to the south. Its muscular invigoration talent had manifested, but as its healing powers were broken, its wielder would always experience awful pain—Willem remembered that guy complaining about it.

Beside it was Mulsum Aurea. A Quasi Brave had brought it along when called up as reinforcements to defend the Brilliant City of Ristiel. Willem had never seen its talent firsthand, but he'd heard it could actually confer temporary immortality.

"…Ha-ha."

What a terrible kind of reunion this was, he thought.

Thud. Not caring if he dirtied the pants of his military uniform, he sat on the spot.

He activated a slight bit of magic and gave his eyes the power of Seeing. There was a sharp pain in the corner of his head, but he didn't pay it any mind.

Yeah, that's what he thought. All the swords were tattered and worn out. Their veins of enchantment had come loose, were cut away, completely in disorder; everything everywhere was all over the place.

Are you still fighting, despite all this?

"—Can I ask you something?"

"What is it?"

"The Carillon are man-made miracles created for emnetwiht by emnetwiht. Only people of the same race with the qualifications to be a Brave can wield them. They should be nothing but museum pieces now. So why are you collecting them? How are you making them fight?"

"Haven't you noticed already?"

"We're Braves, too, right?"

He ignored the voice replaying in the corner of his mind.

"Tell me."

"Sophistry and stretching logic are the basics of magic. Since there are no emnetwiht remaining, we simply need to use a replacement. Those girls are leprechauns—the only race able to use the same tools as the emnetwiht and complete their work. That is the answer to your question."

"...I see."

So that was what was going on.

He lifted himself off the ground and brushed the dust off his bottom. He looked at all the sacred blades lined up in a row.

"So they're your partners now, huh?"

Willem felt lonely but proud, yet sad.

He murmured, a strange mix of feelings inside him.

✝

What am I? Willem thought.

Several things came to mind.

Someone who once wished to be a Legal Brave.

Someone who once lived with a Carillon as a Quasi Brave.

And someone who'd lost that capability at the end of a battle and now lived as an empty shell.

One needed the appropriate background to become a Legal Brave.

Perhaps it would be more appropriate to call it persuasiveness.

Someone born with divine blood, or the descendant of a past Brave, or born on a night of prophecy, or a person whose hometown had been destroyed by a dragon, or the only child who'd inherited a secret martial art, or somebody with a powerful demon sealed inside them.

Real Braves all had backgrounds like that. The only people who could actually gain superpowers were those who others looked at and murmured with a nod, *"I wouldn't be surprised if that guy had superpowers."*

That's why Willem could never become a Legal Brave.

No matter how much he wished, he would never be qualified enough for that.

His birth parents had been ordinary cotton workers. He'd grown up in an orphanage. His life was somewhat unlucky but also somewhat lucky. It was only matter of course that such an unimpressive background would yield him nothing but unimpressive powers. That was something he had no control over and couldn't do anything about.

If only there had been classes for secret sword arts that were easy to learn in his neighborhood, but alas, the world wasn't that convenient.

"You got no talent."

His master at the time had laid it out for him bluntly.

"That Brave salvation system is basically just for the elite. Legendary heroes, half man / half gods, created this system to fight off greater gods and whatever other threats. It's on a total different dimension than things that look for victory in the smallest limits, like our battle techs. Something for people who carry the world's trouble on their own shoulders, people with extraordinary jobs and destinies." He shook his head. *"Those arcane arts, too, aye. Decent folk can't*

even activate 'em, and they wouldn't be able to handle the reaction even if they forced it… Only breaks their body and ends with 'em in no state to fight at all. And Willem, I hate to tell you this, but you're decent folk."

A short silence.

A deep exhale.

"Don't make that face. I'm not giving you a death sentence because I want to. It's a truth I have to tell you and a reality you have to understand. That's all."

He had rejected those words back then.

He'd still refused to give up.

Looking back on it, it might have been childish retaliation. But he had been serious. Willem had not made the decision lightly when he chose to oppose his master, right up until the very end.

He remembered the twentieth Legal Brave, appointed by the Church of Exalted Light.

She had a breathtaking, impressive history.

Not only was she a descendant of the very first Legal Brave, but she had also been born heir to a country of knights. In her ninth autumn, an army of gloom elves attacked her country. Everything precious to her—her parents, her friends, her home—was burned to ash. A loyal retainer spirited her away from the crumbling castle, bringing her to a retired old general who lived in a village far away in the borderlands, where she learned lost sword techniques.

When he'd first heard her story, he could only say, *"Is that so?"*

He had been oddly calm, seeing what kind of person was chosen to be a Legal Brave.

Even when he learned that one of the only five oldest holy blades in the world, Seniorious—the beloved blade of the eighteenth Legal Brave—would be given to her, he'd felt neither happiness nor envy for her.

He stopped thinking about how the more he compared these tales of another world to himself, the more miserable he became.

*   *   *

It was only a long time afterward that he came to realize.

There was a reason these people could fight. They had a reason to fight. They had reasons they had to fight. That's why no one had noticed, including themselves. They'd taken it as a given and had never even imagined it.

That girl. The twentieth Legal Brave.

She who had been born with the power to strike down demons, who concealed the sadness of losing her family and home, who had taken up a mystical job that had been created long in the past, who carried a shining, holy blade that could even reach the Visitors.

She had never once wished she could fight.

Events had simply created a situation where she had to, so she thrust herself into a war of revenge. Those around her expected it of her, so she'd stood up to the dragons and the gods. She had simply been controlled by the demands of those around her—a puppet with no will.

The moment he realized that, Willem hated her.

He'd thought he could never forgive her.

And in truth…even now, those feelings still lingered.

The sun was setting.

A light rain began to fall.

"Should've brought an umbrella…"

Though those words quietly escaped his lips, he didn't feel like taking shelter from the rain or returning to his room.

Island No. 68, the harbor.

Everything necessary for airships to come and go was stored there—the doorway to the island.

He stood by the edge as droplets pelted his body.

Several torn cotton clouds were visible floating below him. And spreading out far beneath that, he could see what had once been the surface. The green of the trees, the azure of rivers and oceans, even the yellow of sand and stone no longer existed. All he could see was a strange, muddied gray dust that covered everything.

He'd come out here to see this view. He wanted to confirm the things he had lost and could never get back.

But even that gray was melting into the darkness of night as though being chased by the setting sun.

Several things now made sense.

For example, venenum handling.

Venenum was like heat.

By calling the flame of magic into his heart, he could set it ablaze, and returning that to the outside world was how he used his power. This heat, however, taxed the user's body. Even if the user tried to gain an even more powerful fire, their own life force would hold them back. That was what decided the upper limits of how much venenum any person could wield, and it varied between races.

That was why odd life-forms unconcerned with their personal well-being could wield such immense power that no other race could replicate.

That power, which probably wasn't kept in check, could go destabilize and detonate. The resulting explosion would be big enough to blow away both the user and their enemies, creating a gigantic crater in the battlefield and leaving behind nothing but a single Carillon in the center.

"Sure makes for excellent weapons—"

They were entirely disposable bombs.

It might not be an entirely efficient way of using this energy, but there was a great meaning and value in having that option itself.

There was one other thing that made sense.

Willem had thought, *Man, I bet these guys are strong,* when he first heard about them.

A race that specialized in war. A life-form whose destiny was simply striving for victory.

What excellent persuasiveness. That was the only job they carried with them, and he had no room to complain.

Those girls would be perfect inheritors of the title of Legal Brave.

Though he could never become one, they could do it for him.

Wonderful. What a joyous thing it was. They must surely be hoping for the same, too. In that case, he should be happy for them. He should give them his blessing.

Woo-hoo, that's great!

I'll leave everything to you, good luck!

"—I wanna die."

Of course, he knew. He wouldn't grumble about this.

The ugly side of his warped disposition, swollen to the point of oblivion, was running around in circles inside his mind.

He was thinking peculiar things only because he was alone in that place. It would be more gracious of him if he just went to the girls—rather, the faeries—and told them how he felt.

But he couldn't do something like that. Unrelated outsiders should never complicate the battles for which the Braves were preparing.

"—Hmm?"

A light pierced the sea of clouds above his head and entered his vision.

An airship was approaching.

The light was so bright, he couldn't make out the silhouette very well. But he could at least tell it wasn't a commuter airship or a ferryman's airship.

It was small, but it was probably a military transport ship.

The heavy sound of metal resounded as the vehicle moored at the port.

The impact deck groaned slightly. Three anchor arms were fixed in place, from back to front. The two rotor blades gradually came to a stop. The booming, running sound of the enchanted combustion furnace slowly grew quieter.

The exit hatch opened with applied air pressure.

Two figures emerged from inside the ship.

"You—"

The two figures were girls…leprechauns he knew.

Chtholly and Ithea.

Both of them wore clothes he didn't recognize—a woman's informal military uniform.

Something was strange. Ithea wore a grim expression on her face while an exhausted Chtholly leaned on her as they walked.

"…Well, well. Good evenin', Second Enchantments Officer Willem." Ithea looked at him, only her speech reminiscent of her usual self. "This is a strange place to meet. Out for a walk in the rain?"

She was mostly right. Maybe she'd purposefully said something off topic as a joke, as a way to gloss over the situation.

But regardless, he honestly couldn't let them deceive him now.

"You two, what in the world are—?"

"Well, I suppose you could say the same for us. We just went for a little stroll off the island…but you wouldn't believe me if I said that, huh?"

"You're damn well right. This is—"

Willem faltered.

He hesitated as to whether or not he should ask now. Yet—

"You were off fighting, weren't you? With the Seventeen Beasts."

"Nya-ha-ha, so you knew? How embarrassing."

Chtholly didn't respond. When he tried to approach, wondering if she had been hurt that badly, there was more.

"Um, no thank you. There's nothing for you to do, Officer. If you're going to ask, then if you could please, take care of this." Ithea's eyes briefly flitted behind her.

He saw a mountain.

The mountain was covered entirely in milky-white scales. It wore a military uniform. Slowly, it shrunk down and squeezed itself out of the airship.

Eyes near the top of the mountain peak peeled open and glared down at Willem.

—I've seen this guy once, this lizardfolk.

"That uniform. Ssso you are Willem."

His voice hissed, like a threatening snake.

Lizardfolk throats differed greatly from those of other races. So when they spoke the official language of the island cluster, their pronunciation was peculiar.

"...Yeah. And you?"

He ignored Willem's question and said, "Carry these." He practically threw two long, thin objects at him.

The lizardfolk's actions seemed so natural, Willem didn't think too much about it and reflexively extended his hand. But while the load was nothing for a lizardfolk's fantastic physical strength, it was much too heavy for the muscles of a regular emnetwiht.

Willem couldn't catch them, and the things fell to the ground. There was the grating sound of metal.

"...This is..."

There were two large swords, securely wrapped in white cloth.

"Thessse are their weaponss. Return them to sstorage." That was all the lizardfolk said before returning to the airship.

"H-hey!"

"I have nothing to sssay to you. Thosse who are not warriorss may not enter placcess where warriorss ssstand."

The door closed, swallowing the boulder-like back.

"Ahhh. Don't mind him. That's just how he, I mean, Mr. Lizard is." Ithea spoke lightly. "And while you're not minding him, it'd be a big help if you carried those swords. As you can see, my hands are pretty full helping Chtholly."

"...Is she injured?"

"Nah, she just got too into it and became dizzy. Well, if we just dump her in the infirmary, she'll wake up eventually."

"I see."

He lifted one of fallen swords from the ground.

It was a sensation he hadn't felt in a long time, one he knew even through the thick fabric. Even in the faint light, there was no mistaking it.

"Seniorious…right?"

"Oh? Surprised you know."

Of course he knew. He was a Quasi Brave who had lived through a time when everyone recognized that name.

A swing to the right cut down dragons. A swing to the left sliced through gods. The very first created even when counting among the Carillon. The golden-bronze dragon slayer. The deity crusher. The secret blade within the plain scabbard. Its various nicknames together could fill an entire book—the holy sword of holy swords carried much history and achievement.

The beloved companion of both the eighteenth and the twentieth Legal Braves—the symbol of heroism itself.

"Is he yours?"

"Nope, that's Chtholly's. The one I'm compatible with is the other one," she said, and as if he just remembered, he scooped up the second.

"Valgulious."

"Sure is. What, you sure know a lot all of a sudden. Did you read our inventory list or something?"

"No." He shook his head. "It's a coincidence that I happen to know a lot of swords."

"Hmm, I'm not sure what kind of humility that is." Ithea tilted her head.

"Give me that, too."

"Huh? Oh, wait—"

He scooped up Chtholly, who was still limp, and put her on his back.

Behind them, there was a shrill sound of metal. The airship was taking off from the port.

"…You're stronger than I thought." Ithea, now with nothing to carry, waved both her hands as she mumbled.

"It's my job to support you."

"Wow, you sure sound cool."

Willem started walking first. Ithea followed a half step behind him.

"So. How much did you learn about us?"

"…I don't know anything. All I know is that faeries use the Carillon…I mean, dug weapons…to fight to protect the islands. Something like that."

"Oohh, that's pretty close to a bull's-eye," Ithea said absently. She looked up to the sky. "It didn't freak you out? Our lives are disposable. We use the legacy or whatever left behind by those dreadful emnetwiht. Even I think it's a pretty nasty setting."

"Don't call it a setting."

Yeah, she's right. That's exactly what it is.

To put it simply, Braves needed precisely those kinds of settings. The sadder, the better. The more miserable, the more ideal it was. They became stronger through a multitude of settings that would be their job or fate or destiny or whatever. Then, those qualities would simply be reduced to power for controlling the emnetwiht's legacies.

Whether they wished for it or not, they had nothing to do with those circumstances.

"—A long time ago, I knew people in a situation similar to yours."

"Ooh, an old tale? Are you trying to seduce me?"

"It's not long enough to be a tale. I owed a lot to them. So when I heard about you guys, I just couldn't leave it alone. That's all."

"Wow, that was short."

"I said it wasn't gonna be long."

"I guess you did," she said in a flat tone, kicking a pebble at her feet. "Doesn't it feel like this is the part where you confide in me and tell me everything, and we start establishing our love for each other? I mean, we're all the way out here, just the two of us."

"Did you forget the third person on my back?"

"Chtholly's, like, the person who wakes up in the middle of it all and watches. Then we start a beautiful love triangle of adoration and jealousy."

"What've you been reading recently?"

"Bursting Triad."

He'd heard that title before. It was a novel that took place on a fictitious island. If he remembered correctly, more than half the characters in the book repeat a cycle of cheating and adultery in the name of pursuing true love.

Now it made sense. He'd wondered how this group of girls (and Nygglatho) learned generalities about society living by themselves in the forest, and romances were one way to gain knowledge (albeit biased) of the outside world.

"Especially the third book. That is *so* good."

"I'm confiscating that. That's not something for kids to read."

"That's tyranny! Who are you calling a kid?! Wait, you know what it is just by hearing the title?!"

On Island No. 28, in all its decadent charm, there was a constant influx of pleasures coming from all different islands. And as Willem went from day job to day job, he'd merely happened to overhear such information. That was all.

In the meantime, he decided to brush off Ithea's complaints and questions.

"Don't be so loud. You'll wake her up."

As his back swayed slightly, he heard a slight groan.

4. The Valiant and Their Successors

What am I? Willem thought.

He wasn't a Brave anymore, had no more reason to fight for this shrunken world, and lacked the power to do so.

So all that remained was a flimsy weapons manager.

Someone whose only responsibility was to stay there, like a decoration.

He could disappear at any time. It wouldn't hurt anyone. An invisible ghost.

Ten minutes later, in the infirmary.

"Why are you here?"

That was the first thing Chtholly said after regaining consciousness.

"I can't stay by the sick?"

"Who are you calling sick?"

Her face still flushed, her voice caused her lips to actively pout.

"You, obviously. Did you know? The old Braves, the ones you're emulating, would get extra pay if they got specified illnesses or injuries while on duty. Right at the top of that list was acute venenum poisoning—what you have right now."

"...I don't get your jokes sometimes."

She turned away in a huff.

It wasn't a joke, but Willem wouldn't mind if she didn't believe him.

"Come on, look at me. Let me change the towel on your forehead."

"No."

"That's not something for the sick to decide."

"It doesn't bother me. This always happens, and it goes away if I rest a little bit."

"Don't be silly." He smacked his forehead lightly. "You have to completely drain the poison every time; otherwise, it'll keep coming back. You'll reach your limit fast if you just treat it like that."

"Wow, you sound like a specialist."

"I am a specialist. I'm an enchantments officer."

"Hmph." Chtholly's eyes turned away again, as though she didn't want to listen to him.

Actual enchantments officers were originally meant to work the general forging and regulating enchanted machines that supported operations on the battlefield, just as the title implied. A second officer had power and responsibility that rivaled the superior. And of course, a high degree of education and training were generally required in order to reach this position through normal channels.

Willem, however, didn't have such a past as a member of the Guard. What he mentioned was nothing but a front and didn't correspond with his actual power—this was common knowledge among the faeries.

"I'm the manager. At least let me worry."

"I don't... It doesn't matter if you're a manager or whatever. You don't have to worry about me."

She didn't look at him. He couldn't see her face.

For the time being, he could see her ears were red, so her fever probably hadn't gone down yet.

"It's just… Limits and stuff, none of that matters. I don't have any time left anyway."

"Time? What are you talking about?"

"Hey, let me ask you something." Ignoring the confusion in his voice, she responded by queuing up a question of her own.

"What?"

"If. Just if. If I were to die in five days, would you be nicer to me?"

…Silence.

"What?" Unsure exactly what she was after, he inadvertently responded with another question.

"Just answer, even if it's hypothetical. Would you ask me about my final wish and stuff?"

"Wait. Five days? Where did that come from? You need to tell me more about this; otherwise, I can't answer."

"Five days from today, big Six, Timere, will attack Island No. 15."

Another silence.

"None of the Seventeen Beasts can fly. That's why Regule Aire stays afloat, even after everything on the surface was destroyed. But only Timere, the hidden Beast No. 6, can both leave itself on the surface and still attack Regule Aire. Its two powers are ripping itself apart and growing rapidly. It can leave its main body down below while tearing into millions of tiny pieces, then let those bits get carried away by the wind. It waits to be lifted onto an island by chance. When it gets there, it'll grow incredibly fast, absorbing and destroying the island in six to eight hours."

Silence.

"Of course, Regule Aire has a way to fight this. An interference as big as a Beast would absolutely trigger tactical precognition before it reached the islands. The stronger the fragment, the faster the forecast. And of course, it's also possible to take preventative measures and prepare for such a thing. That's how Regule Aire has managed to avoid many attacks from Timere. For hundreds of years."

Silence.

"About six months ago, they foresaw a particularly large fragment coming. They identified its scale pretty accurately, too. The normal firepower they could deploy to the scene would be no match for it. But a faerie with a dug weapon—"

"—Could defeat it in exchange for her life?"

"...Right. I'd heard it was the perfect size for Seniorious, and I'm supposed to defeat it with a self-destruct suicide attack. As luck would have it." Chtholly shrugged her shoulders on the bed.

There could be no preferable outcome than the sacrifice of just one person. If her power was insufficient, even by a little, then they would lose a second or third faerie, too. That would probably end up being either Ithea or Nephren—

"Of course, it's just an example."

Slowly, Chtholly turned to him.

A mischievous grin. But the smile never reached her eyes.

"Well? If something like that happened, would you listen to my final wish and stuff?"

"Depends on the wish."

"That's, um, well, for example...," she mumbled, her words faltering. "...Like, if I asked you to kiss me, would you?"

Her too?

He considered that it was probably his turn to get flustered or blush, but as Willem didn't feel like doing any of that, he groaned. "You're saying you have five days left to live, and *that's* what you ask for?"

"I-is that bad?"

He created a circle with his thumb and middle finger. He tensed his middle finger, leveling it close to her forehead...

"Owwww!!"

He flicked her.

"Stop acting like a cheeky kid. You've been reading too many of those romance books."

"N-no, I haven't, I've been reading other kinds of books, too!"

So she isn't going to deny reading romances.

The things Chtholly was saying were growing odd, either due to her fever or because she was honestly becoming flustered. Not only that, she hadn't noticed what she was doing yet.

"Wh-what's wrong with wanting to create some final memories anyway?"

She was probably doing it unconsciously, tightly clenching the silver brooch he'd noticed her wearing a few times before.

"Even if you'll be gone, you wouldn't want to disappear, at least, right? You'd want someone to remember you. You'd want someone to be connected with you."

Tears welled up in her eyes.

"What's wrong with that?"

"I didn't say that. You're making an irrational leap to say it's wrong."

He placed his hand on her forehead. It was hot.

"I'm saying, don't sell yourself short by being so desperate that you'd be fine with anyone. Doing that with whoever happens to be nearby will just end badly for you."

"I don't care, so come buy it all up while things are cheap! It's fundamental smart shopping to not let a good opportunity to buy pass!"

"This isn't shopping with the missus, geez. And if you want to cry, then cry as much as you can while someone's by your side. Only experts know how to stop crying when they're alone. I can't really recommend it to a novice."

"Shut up. You're not gonna kiss me, so no talking. I am not crying."

"It sounds like you are?"

"I'm not." She insisted stubbornly.

What was I? Willem wondered.

He checked over and over. He was a shell of a Brave who'd lost everything he wanted to protect.

Shells didn't wish for anything. They didn't have that power.

"...Honestly." Willem scratched his head. "Just lie down for a second."

"No." Chtholly turned away in a huff.

"Just listen to me."

"No."

"I swear, you're so stubborn."

He gripped Chtholly's shoulder forcefully and turned her toward him.

As he did, he drew closer and lightly pressed his lips against the girl's forehead.

"Huh?"

Chtholly's entire body suddenly froze.

A great shock caused her brain to reflexively turn on its limiters. Chtholly was unable to process what just happened to her forehead. She only knew that her body had been startled by something, and she locked up.

The sensation she should have felt on her forehead hadn't reached her brain at all.

"Now I think you'll listen. Hurry up and lie down."

"What? Hold on. What was that? I don't really know."

"Hurry up."

Willem snapped his fingers on both hands.

He gripped her shoulder and flipped her over.

"Ahhh!"

"It might be a little overbearing, but your fever will go down. Close your mouth, just in case."

"M-my mouth? Huh? What does that mean?"

He placed his hand on her back and felt around her muscles and blood with his index finger.

One characteristic of victims suffering venenum poisoning was that body tissue still active with venenum could lose its functions. So sometimes, the body acted on the assumption it had caught some sort of terrible disease, resulting in a high fever. Symptoms of that sort were common.

However, on the flip side, if Willem could examine her properly like this, he could see where her venenum was pooling.

"Here...and here."

"Eeee!!"

He pressed down firmly with his finger.

Having been a Quasi Brave as long as he was, it wasn't unusual for either Willem or his companions to get venenum poisoning. And there were many times when they'd been forced to somehow alleviate the symptoms while still on the battlefield so they could continue fighting.

It was insanely important to prevent their strength from being whittled down in a long battle. That was why Willem had latched on to busy field medics and forced them to teach him this technique.

"Ow, that hurts!!"

"Your venenum is coagulated in your muscles, that's why. You'll feel better when I loosen it."

"I know, but ah! That's tickli—!"

"Stop moving so much. Stay still."

"I said, I know, but… Hn, hnng, mmm…"

The "points" were ten spots that ran parallel to one another along either side of the spine.

One by one, he went to each and loosened them with his index finger.

It was like he was pushing through the pools of venenum with healthy blood.

To put it bluntly, the sensation was very similar to relieving stiff muscles with a massage. Well, besides the need to prepare for it beforehand by stimulating pressure points, it was practically the same.

"Haaah…"

He found tiny points of pooled venenum and forced their movement.

At the next point, he did the same thing.

He must have been doing that for ten minutes.

After finishing the treatment, Willem finally released the girl's body. The majority of the venenum knots had been loosened. As strength returned to Chtholly's muscles and her blood flow normalized, the body would be able to clear the rest of the venenum on its own.

"All right, that should be good enough."

Chtholly, having been tossed around by the storm-like stimulus, was spent of energy and stared blearily. Willem pulled the blanket over her back.

"Now, just rest. You should be feeling much better in the morning."

"Ohay…"

Her response was inarticulate, probably because she still wasn't fully conscious. She would probably knock out on her own soon enough if he just left her be. That wasn't a problem, at least.

He left Chtholly alone, her breathing still ragged, and exited the infirmary.

†

What am I? Willem wondered.

But it quickly became a pain, so he stopped. He had other things to think about now.

†

Paper. Paper. Paper.

That was the first thing that caught his eye when he entered the room.

It was also the second thing and the third thing he noticed.

He took a half step back and double-checked the room's plaque. Engraved there on the bronze sheet was, without a doubt, MATERIAL ROOM.

Once again, he went inside. It was by no means a small room, but it was jam-packed with paper. Not only that, but the variation was astounding. Applications to have the toilet repaired in the faerie warehouse, instructions for coordinating with the other races on the unified front against the Seventeen Beasts, an order form for a big bag of carrots and potatoes, a nighttime patrol report, clippings from a girls' magazine—and it was all jumbled together in one big pile.

Tick, tick, tick. The second hand on the clock on the wall echoed loudly in his ears.

"…This place is a *mess*."

Paper rustled as he made his way through it, searching for a desk and chair. He placed the stack that was on the chair aside for the time being, plopped into the seat, and looked around the room.

"This place is a *mess*," he murmured again.

He sat for a while with his arms folded, thinking about where he should begin.

He came to the conclusion that he would not reach any conclusions thinking about it.

He reached out to the nearest pile and pulled out a sheet from the bottommost layer. It was a letter detailing the results of an equipment inspection ten years past.

I see. Sediment from a decade ago.

He felt a little like an archaeologist.

But it would be a waste of time if he let it overwhelm him like this. For now, he would start with sorting everything out—but as he reached out to the nearest tower, he realized there was someone peeking into the room from beside the door.

It was a faerie with ashen hair. Her enigmatic gaze focused squarely on him.

Thinking she might need to do something in the room, he waited. But she didn't respond. The way she stuck by the side of the door and continued staring at him without so much as a stir gave her the appearance of a sculpture.

"You need something, Nephren?"

"Not really."

Nephren responded with an indifferent tone, then turned on her heel and disappeared.

"…What was that all about?"

He tilted his head as he faced the room again.

There was something he wanted to know. More than likely, what he sought was sunken somewhere in this ocean of paper.

The clock on the wall chimed twelve times in a row.

The date had changed.

*   *   *

Even after spending so much time, all Willem had managed to do was put the bundles of paper on the desk in order.

There was no doubt his search was going to take all night. But it was also pretty unlikely it was going to lead to anything, even if he kept working without stopping to sleep.

"...I'm exhausted."

Now that he thought about it, he hadn't considered food.

The last time he'd eaten had been before noon, so he calculated he'd spent more than half a day going full speed ahead without any nutritional intake.

When he realized that, his stomach grumbled.

"Man..."

Had he noticed a little earlier, he might have been able to ask for a snack in the dining hall...but regretting that now wouldn't fill his stomach.

Willem lay his head on the desk.

He closed his eyes.

Regardless of his empty stomach, if he kept chugging along while ignoring his exhaustion, the only thing he'd accomplish would be the loss of his ability to concentrate. He figured he could keep going after a quick rest. He would close his eyes, just until the clock chimed again.

...The smell of coffee tickled his nose.

The sound of a cup being placed onto the desk rang in his ears.

It was a gift, he thought. He remembered he'd left the door open.

"Oh, thanks—"

Just as he was going to say Nygglatho's name, he saw who was standing there. Wavy, light-gray hair. Charcoal eyes that felt distant and were hard to tell where they were looking.

"—Nephren?"

"Ren is fine."

"Oh, okay. Thanks, Ren."

He looked at the desk again; right next to the coffee sat a simple sandwich on a plate. Willem was truly thankful.

"I haven't done anything to warrant your thanks." Her distant gaze scanned the room. "I just came to see because I was curious. What are you doing?"

"Hmm, just trying to find something."

"Here?"

"Yes, here. Treasure chests are always hiding in the deepest part of underground labyrinths. You've gotta be ready for some hardship if you want to find anything of value."

"...Mm."

He took a sip of the coffee.

"It's sweet."

There was a huge amount of sugar in it, almost to the point of giving the coffee a syrupy texture.

"I thought you might be tired. You don't like sweet things?"

"Nah, I like it."

He drained the whole cup. Nephren's eyes wavered in slight surprise.

Then he stuffed the sandwich into his mouth. Roasted dovelet, slightly wilted lettuce on dried bread. There might've been a bit too much mustard on it, but it was just the thing he needed to replenish his tired body.

"Phew."

Willem breathed.

His body was the capricious sort and eating even a tiny bit of food immediately revived some strength.

"So."

Nephren placed both hands on the desk, assuming a pressing pose with her expressionless face, and she questioned him.

"What are you looking for so late?"

"Uhh... Well, I guess there's no need to hide it. Your mission records."

"Mm?" She tilted her head. "Why?"

"I'm an outsider, a fake officer, on top of being out of time. There's too much I don't know. I could also ask Nygglatho, but she's not from the Guard, which means I won't necessarily learn anything useful from her perspective. So it'd be best if I check the Guard's data with my own eyes."

"From the perspective of a fake officer?"

"Through the lens of my old experiences, I guess you could say."

"…Mm?" Her head tilted in the other direction.

"Don't think too much about it. Everyone has a past."

"Okay." She nodded obediently. "Is there anything you want me to do?"

"Would that be okay? In that case, see if you can find documents detailing the frequency of Timere's appearances, the mission timing and deployment of all troops over the past ten years, as well as records detailing decisive losses. Also, if you can, records of attempts to repair and adjust the Cari…dug weapons. Anything that talks about what they were aiming for or what they did, plus the results. That would be ideal."

"That's very specific."

"I'll take care of all the detailed checks. All you need to do is find and pick out things that look like they might be related."

"Understood."

Now that he'd fortified himself with food, the work started anew. Willem rolled up his sleeves. A moment later, Nephren followed his lead and did the same.

Facing the ocean of overflowing paper, the two sailors began to row.

Dawn broke.

The two sailors were shipwrecked spectacularly in the endless paper seas.

Morning came.

Chtholly Nota Seniorious woke the same time she always did. Sluggishly pulling herself out of bed, she soon realized that she wasn't in her own room, grasped that this was the infirmary, thought about why she might be in a place like this, and tried to recall what had happened the night before.

She remembered.

Her brain boiled over in a flash.

"Wh—?! Wha-wha-wha-wha—?"

She had been inebriated by her fever. She had been weak. She had lost all proper judgment. Under normal circumstances, there was no way she would have said or done any of those things.

She could think of several excuses. Even all of those combined could not overrule the reality of what had happened.

"If I were to die in five days, would you be nicer to me?"

"Wh-wh-what on earth was I saying——?!"
She dove backward straight into the bed she'd just climbed out of.

She rolled, flipped, kicked, and generally went wild. The bed creaked loudly under her, but that wasn't something that bothered her right now.

"...Like, if I asked you to kiss me, would you?"

"Gyaaaaaahh!!"
She hugged the pillow, squeezing it with all her might. She punched it. Then it flew into the wall with a mighty throw.

Why did I say that? I can't think of a reason why. Well, I certainly don't hate him and definitely appreciate him, and I'm aware that I rather like him, but really, that's something totally different, plus liking someone as a person and liking someone as a member of the opposite sex are two completely different things, which by no means should be mixed up at all, but that makes it almost look like I've been crushing on him for a while, and the fever made me confess my love to him, and aghhhhhh, okay, I'm not going to think about that anymore.

There was one more thing. Chtholly's memory was fuzzy after a certain point, but she felt like things had gotten intense. He'd definitely said it was to relieve her fever—

"Chtholly!! Are you okay?!"

"Yawha?!"
There was a sudden voice, and flustered, she hid her face in the blankets.

"Ohh, she's fine."

"U-um. Yesterday, I heard you came back really tired, so I wanted to see if you're doing okay. Do you want to eat anything?"

Judging by the voices and the presences, she had two visitors.

"Collon…and Lakhesh…?"

She slowly peeked out from under the blanket, confirming who was there.

No doubt. She could only see two very bright shades of pink and peach.

"Hmm? Your face is red." Pink-haired Collon peered at her.

"R-really? Isn't that just your imagination?"

Chtholly looked away.

"But it looks like you're all right physically. Whenever you and the others come back from fighting, you always seem to be in so much pain. I'm glad you're okay today." That was peach-haired Lakhesh.

"—Huh?"

Now that she mentioned it, her body felt oddly light.

Last night, she had definitely worked her venenum to the point of passing out. In the past, the morning after days she did that, she had always been bothered by heavy fatigue.

She got out from bed and hopped gingerly in place.

Rather than fatigued, her body felt incredibly good. She had recovered as if magic had been cast on her.

"You're right. I feel so spry."

"Spirit and guts!"

That…probably wasn't it.

"Did you not notice?"

"Uh, well…" She wondered why this was. Maybe it was the result of that odd massage—the details of which she would try not to remember, since her head still felt like it was about to explode. "…Oh, right. Do you know where he is?"

"He?" Lakhesh stumbled for a second. "If you mean Mr. Willem, then the last time I saw him, he was in the material room."

"The material room… You mean the paper storage?"

What did he have to do there?

Just as she said, it was a place where they just tossed bundles of paper. At the very least, it wasn't somewhere useful for looking up documents. As no one ever went near it, faeries often used it to hide when skipping out on cleaning duty.

"He was with Nephren."

"…Huh?"

"Collon!" Lakhesh raised her voice critically, but Collon paid no mind.

"They were sleeping on the sofa together," she continued. She shouldn't have.

"…Uh-huh." Chtholly tilted her head. "Sure. Okay."

"U-um, Miss Chtholly?"

"I just remembered I have to do something, so I'm going out for a bit. Thanks for checking in on me, and as you can see, I'm fine so don't worry."

"Um, yes, of course, but"—Lakhesh slowly looked up at her with wide eyes—"be gentle with them, okay?"

"What do you mean?"

Chtholly smiled and left the infirmary.

They were lucky to have excavated a sofa as they worked. Willem had plopped down onto it, and a woozy Nephren lay her head on his lap.

"…Well, at least we got something usable out of this," he murmured softly to himself so as not to wake his partner. He held a small stack of paper in his hand. It wasn't as much as he'd hoped to find, and there were many unexpected things mixed in, but he managed to excavate a sizable portion of the information he was searching for.

He picked out one paper from among the sheaf. He glanced over an account describing the existence of faeries.

Faeries took many forms. There were blurred will-o'-the-wisps that led people lost in the forests astray. Then came the children with wings, halos of light glowing around them. And finally, little people, who only came up to a person's knee.

Faeries were all elusive beings, loved trickery, had the ability to use

several forms of mysterious "magic," resided in forests as well as their own kingdoms…and in most cases, they took an interest in emnetwiht and were always poking their noses in emnetwiht business.

Well…that sounds about right. Those are the kinds of faeries that I know.

But something was off. Willem wondered why these children were called leprechauns, these children who looked *exactly* like emnetwiht girls aside from the color of their hair. But there were many more important things he needed to learn before that, so he left it for later.

I did think they might have evolved in these past five hundred years, but…

As he pondered absently, he continued reading.

The basic theory of necromancy was spelled out. It was a compilation of very occult logic, based on the premise that the soul existed. In essence, it stated that the spirit is pure white in the very beginning and then dyed the color of the world as it goes through life after birth. In conclusion, it takes longer for the soul to finish growing through its interaction with life than the physical body. Even if babies and children had mature bodies, their souls differed vastly from those of adults.

And so souls that lost their physical bodies before they were completely dyed in the world's colors become inconsistencies and "die before they are finished being born." Usually, according to the rules of this world, souls would then go to the afterlife (*if such a thing really did exist*), but the souls of those who died too soon lost sight of where they needed to pass and wandered in place.

Those were faeries.

Lost souls that perished when they were too young to understand their own death.

So their actions conformed to the behavior of babies and children. Led by their curiosity, unaffected by good or evil, sometimes innocent and sometimes cruel, they play tricks over and over in attempts to get closer to people.

"And yet, they have no place to call their own in this world… Huh…"

Willem glanced down at the girl on his lap.

His focus returned to the document.

Everything written afterward made him feel sick. It was basically a detailed method of artificially creating faeries and how to use them. When it started talking about sacrifice, he stopped reading. He hadn't picked this up to become a necromancer anyway.

He moved on to the second document. It was a report detailing the mission of a faerie he didn't know. The Carillon she took with her was Insania. She'd fought desperately against three parts of Six on the verge of losing control of her venenum, yet she'd somehow managed return alive. His eyes continued to quickly scan the words. There were several similar reports in a row. He occasionally read the phrase, "Open the gates to the faerie homeland," which probably referenced a deliberate self-destruction via venenum overload.

Faeries, and thus the leprechaun girls, were, in the strictest sense, not alive. They were ghosts. They didn't count as soldiers, even if they were a part of an army. If any of them perished in battle, they would not be counted among the dead.

"So they're treated like weapons and not like soldiers…hmm," he murmured absently, lightly stroking the gray hair on his lap. He heard a small groan. He thought for a moment he'd woken the girl but then realized he could still hear her soft snoring.

What am I? Willem wondered.

All the answers he could find to that question were lies.

He had to decide here and now. Who was he, right at this moment?

Was he just a shell with no place in this age? Was he a Quasi Brave, thrown out of time, whose dreams had been shattered and who'd lost everything? Was he a flimsy second officer who could just earn money and spend the days as he pleased? Or—

A ray of light slipped through the window.

The sky was covered in rain clouds, like always.

The morning glow poked through the gaps.

Willem unconsciously narrowed his eyes at the brightness.

He felt like he could see someone he hadn't for a long time just beyond it.

"…I just wanted to quickly pay off my debt and head over there," he muttered with a dry smile.

"*Shut up. Just do everything you can,*" replied the person beyond the light…or so he felt.

Ah, damn it. Hell. Don't do this.

How do you think I've felt this year and a half?

He scratched his head.

"…Willem?"

His name came from his lap.

"Oh, you're up. Thanks. You helped me find a lot."

"…I haven't done anything to warrant your thanks." She nimbly turned over on the sofa. "I just reached out because you looked like you would shrivel up if I left you alone."

"Still, thanks."

He patted her small head and ruffled her gray hair vigorously.

"Gh—"

She grimaced in annoyance, but she didn't bat his hand away.

"All right, we should get up now. We have a guest."

"Wh—?!"

A surprised voice came from the half-open door.

The door creaked slightly. Through the gap, they could see Chtholly, who seemed upset somehow, her eyes narrowed.

"…Um, good morning."

"Morning. How are you feeling?"

"Huh? Uh, uhm, right. Really good, I think."

"That's good. I realized later that I'd never tried that on a child before, so I was a little worried that it might be a little too effective."

"Guh…"

It looked like she bent backward, taking damage.

"And hmm… Well, you're right on time, so I want to check something out. Come on, Ren, move your head. It's morning."

"Ngah—"

Willem dropped Nephren's head onto the sofa and stood up.

"So, Chtholly. I hate to ask just after you've gotten better, but come with me for my morning exercises."

She stared up at him blankly, blinking.

✝

The whimsical sky had cleared at some point and become pure blue.

"…Huh?"

Chtholly stood in the middle of the field.

A short distance away, Willem was doing light stretches in loose casual clothes.

Then, before her, Nephren held out a long, thin bundle of fabric—no doubt a dug weapon was inside.

She looked back and forth between Nephren and the bundle, then took it.

It had a familiar feel and weight. If she peeled back the fabric, underneath would be a familiar silvery-white blade. It was currently the dug weapon with the strongest magical resonance factor on Regule Aire—Seniorious.

Why had she been given it at this moment?

"Chtholly, do you like the little ones here?"

"Huh?"

"Are you ready to die to protect their future?"

"That…that doesn't really matter."

In a broad sense, Willem was right. But she didn't feel like she could honestly recognize that. The whole whirlpool of emotions inside her could not so easily be summarized in a word that also included what she was ready for, and she didn't want to allow herself to use the little ones as an excuse for her death.

"I see. Well, that's fine."

Willem also removed the cloth from the dug weapon in his hand.

What emerged was definitely…mass-produced. There were a number of similarly standardized weapons that had been excavated, and their abilities were consistently one rank below the rest.

"Show me the strength I've been hearing about. Come at me."

"WH-WHAT?!"

Chtholly doubted her ears. With their dug weapons, they ranked among the best defense forces in Regule Aire. Basically, she was ludicrously strong. Even lizardfolk armed to the teeth with explosives were no match for her and the others.

So why?

"Do you even understand any of this? You're making a huge mistake if you think this is an evenly matched fight just because you have a dug weapon. Only us leprechauns can activate them."

"Eh, we'll see about that. The result might surprise you if you try."

"This isn't a joke. Do you want to be put through the grinder?"

"No thanks. That would only make Nygglatho happy."

Well, that was true.

"But you won't need to worry about me like that, not for half a millennium. So just get a move on and come at me."

"…Okay. If you're going that far, then…"

Something chilled in Chtholly's mind.

Now that she thought about it, today wasn't the first day Willem had said odd things. On top of that, there was another matter she had to question him and Nephren about. She didn't think it would be a bad idea to display her strength, just once, before having that talk.

She furtively lit her venenum.

Seniorious, sensing its companion was ready for battle, creaked loudly. The countless cracks running along the face of the blade fissured. Then, the faint light that was the manifestation of magic seeped from it.

The current era's technology was insufficient to understand how dug weapons were made or by what principle they operated. What was decipherable was that dug weapons transformed magic poured into them into power. And that if leprechauns poured all of their magic into them, Six (Timere) could not withstand it. That was enough.

"You said it yourself, so don't wish you hadn't—"

She herself cut off the "Okay?" intended to follow.

Chtholly kicked off the ground.

Her concentration, now enhanced by venenum, altered her entire field of view. The colors of the scenery around her disappeared. She felt impatient, as if pushing through lukewarm water. There must have been some twenty regular steps between them, but now she could easily close that gap in just two strides. Her sharp footfalls left shallow holes in the field, but she didn't care.

It was a complete surprise attack. Willem wasn't ready. She aimed for the mass-produced dug weapon, which sat at the end of his right arm, sticking out idly at his side. Victory would be hers if she could send it flying. She'd end it all before anyone got hurt.

The distance between them vanished. Willem's right arm entered Seniorious's range. No one could keep up with a leprechaun at this speed. Not to mention that Willem, in his formless posture, had no way of escaping or striking back at this range.

—*Slash.*

(...Huh?)

A blade stuck into her lower left side. It continued upward diagonally, toward her right shoulder. It severed her ribs. It sundered her lungs. The golden tip plunged into her heart and easily ripped it apart.

Her concentration, heightened so much that time stretched out, precisely itemized every wound.

Slowly, a red pool erupted, drawing a beautiful arc in the blue sky.

There was a chilling sense of loss, partnered with the suffocating reality of death.

(Wh...at...?)

(No...this...)

(Wh...y...?)

Fragments of words appeared in her mind and disappeared. She was ready to die, but she hadn't imagined it would be here. The emptiness of being attacked off guard was sweet yet cold and unbelievably frightening.

Her eyes, open wide in shock, were filled with nothing but the deep-blue sky spread before her…

She fell backward onto the ground.

"Hugyah!"

A cry that sounded like a crushed cat escaped her lungs.

"…Huh?"

Her arms and legs were spread out wide, and she lay on her back.

She stayed like that for a few seconds, staring up blankly, having completely forgotten herself. She spent her final moments in a reprieve before death absolutely dumbfounded.

Then she finally realized something was wrong.

Cautiously, she moved her arm and patted her side. There was no wound. No blood. No pain. Not a single trace on her body of the atrocity that should have befallen her just now was etched on her body.

"What…was…?"

Slowly, she propped herself up.

Seniorious, which she must have let go of at some point, lay on the ground a little ways away.

"You guys have the Carillon's basic functions figured out all wrong."

When she heard Willem's voice, she whirled around.

The young man with black hair just stood there, relaxed.

"They're not 'convenient ritual weapons that respond to the user's force and turn it into power,' like you think they are. There's no way these weapons, forged by the ridiculously weak emnetwiht to defeat the overwhelmingly strong elves and dragons, are something that simply raises a weakling's power. That gap was overwhelming specifically because it couldn't be bridged with cheap tricks like that."

He just kept on talking and talking. Her blood started to boil.

It almost baffled her why she felt so angry.

She had a hunch she shouldn't listen to the rest of what he had to say.

*   *   *

Concentration. Her vision was overwritten again.

She could throw herself out to grab Seniorious, then keep her stance low and rush Willem.

She couldn't see the attack on her, but she could imagine its nature. It was probably a technique that used her momentum and threw it back at her. All her advantages—the activated dug weapon, quickened senses and judgment through her lit venenum—had completely eliminated in her mind the possibility of Willem responding. She had been struck directly in a blind spot born from pure carelessness. He'd used the power of her normal attack against her. The death she'd hallucinated wasn't just a delusion. It was the very future that would have befallen her had Willem felt like it.

She would accept that. She still didn't quite know why, but this person was an extraordinary master.

That's why—!

But there were certain things she refused to accept. She could not let him deny the way faeries fought with dug weapons or the battles they'd waged clinging to that method.

Chtholly's body moved faster than it normally did. She hated to admit that was probably thanks to Willem, but she was also grateful. She closed the ten paces between them with two steps. She stopped suddenly just before their blades could touch to throw off his timing, then she leaped. Twisting in the air, she aimed for his shoulder with Seniorious in her right hand. But at the same time, she would plant a kick on his side with her left foot, in his blind spot. Her true intention was to land the latter. She eradicated the difference between their strength and physique with her awakened venenum and speed. If she managed to pull this off, the pain would likely render him unconscious, but he wouldn't get it if she didn't do at least that much.

—What?

The momentary question vanished from her mind.

This time, she saw Willem move.

With lazy movements, he stuck his sword into Seniorious's orbit and, with just a little effort, threw off both Seniorious's trajectory and Chtholly's posture ever so slightly. He thrust his left shoulder into the opening he created and gently touched Chtholly's side with his hand.

For a moment, physics broke down.

Chtholly's body distorted by itself, and when she thought she had been twisted, she was flung off in one direction.

What...is...this...?!

Again, she could see the cloudless blue autumn sky.

But something was different from last time. This time, she wasn't dreaming about dying. Her body was somehow still alive.

"Gh...!"

She reached out with her left arm, planting her fingers in the ground in a desperate attempt to stop herself. Her nails left a long, ripping trail in the dirt.

She flipped over, touching her fingertips to the ground, and fixed her posture.

"That was a feat of strength, huh?"

Willem's astonished tone really irritated her.

She was the one who was supposed to be astonished.

"...What's the meaning of this?" she demanded, her voice wavering in frustration.

"Hmm? Which part?" he responded, his expression calm.

He immediately caught on that she had a hundred questions.

No longer inclined to rush him, Chtholly walked straight over to him and swung Seniorious. With a nonchalant "Whoops," Willem stopped the attack with his own sword.

She could see a faint light seeping from the cracks on his sword.

"No matter how hard I try to See, I can't sense any activated venenum coming from you. But this sword is awake. That's against the rules!"

"Hey, I was in the middle of explaining that when you attacked me. Carillons, more than anything, are weapons that *use the strongest powers of those who touch the blade.* The stronger the enemy, the more power they gain. That's why they can challenge dragons. Cut down gods. So it follows that the venenum you used to activate Seniorious activated my Percival to the same level... Now, then."

Something shiver inducing crawled down Chtholly's spine.

An attack was coming. That instinct sped up her thought processes. Color drained from her vision, and her limbs flung her back with all her might. Her momentary evasive maneuver immediately relaxed, and she fell square on her bottom.

In the end, she didn't know if that move had been the right reaction. Willem never moved. He still stood there, his arm sticking out idly with the sword in his hand, and his expression twisted into one of praise.

"You move well. And you're decisive. The amount of venenum energy you have is a big deal, too. Not only that, you also have good instincts. Your tactical moves aren't that great, but you're not fighting against other people, so don't worry about that. And you have an overdrive, which is your trump card... Now I can see how you've managed to come this far on strength alone," he said, tossing his sword away.

Chtholly lifted herself from the ground, furrowing her brows, as it might be some kind of trick.

"That's a relief. You're strong. And you can grow even stronger. That's why...you need to come home," he said, his voice a whisper.

Willem's body slowly leaned, and he fell on his back.

A cloud of dust puffed up around him. Chtholly stayed on guard. She cautiously continued staring at the sword that had been tossed away while Willem's two legs pointed straight at her, his arms spread to embrace the sky, and his glassy eyes stared up into the heavens.

...Glassy eyes?

No sooner had Chtholly realized that something felt off than Nephren ran over and checked his heartbeat and pulse.

"Ah!" The other girl didn't sound surprised at all.

"Wh-what is it?" Chtholly asked, her posture still guarded.

Willem had surprised her enough already. Whatever her friend had to say now wouldn't faze her. So she wouldn't faint if anything caught her by surprise. As she told herself all this, she held Seniorious at the ready.

"He's dying," Nephren said quietly.

"Huh?" Her voice was completely clueless.

5. The Strong, Mechanized Woman

On the other side of the communication crystal was the face of a boulder-like lizardfolk.

"There have been no changess to our forecassst. We sshhall vissit the universsse I alerted you to previousssly. We musst quickly releassse the eagle and ssharpen our arrowheadsss."

A lizardfolk characteristic was their roundabout way of speaking, as was how difficult they were to understand when they spoke the official language of the island cluster. It would be very hard for someone unused to it to grasp their meaning.

This is a broad interpretation:

"There have been no changes to our forecast. The attack will take place at the time and place we previously predicted. We must quickly prepare the battlefield and ready our forces."

"…Hmm, all right, then. I mean, all right," Nygglatho responded, sputtering at him.

The enemy moving as predicted meant that all their movements would be as planned.

Can't we do this without having to use these "arrowheads"?!

If she relaxed even the slightest, her mouth would shout what she was thinking of its own accord.

That was why Nygglatho shoved all her feelings deep inside herself. In a corner of her mind, she constructed a different self…an identity that was perceptive, able to choose the best option without hesitation, a machine that could act without being thrown off by her spineless emotions. Then she let that self do all the talking.

"In three days at the eighth bell, we will dispatch three of our current five dug weapon–compatible personnel along with swords from this island are-port."

Aren't you all soldiers?! Warriors?! Don't you eat knowing you will fight at the front lines with the possibility of dying?! Then why don't any of yours die?! Why is it always our girls who end up victims?!

"One of ours, the spirit compatible with dug weapon Seniorious—faerie soldier Chtholly Nota Seniorious—will be opening the gates to the faerie homeland as we enact our strategy."

I can't believe this is your best effort! It can't be! Fight like your life means it! Think of something better! Fight a different way! Save my kids!

"We will suppose that the other two—faerie soldiers Ithea Myse Valgulious and Nephren Ruq Insania—will be standing ready as reserve forces. In the event that the battle is not resolved once Seniorious opens the gates, they will use their judgment to engage with their dug weapons."

They've never known love. They've never known happiness. Why does it all have to end like this?!

"The Orlandry Alliance Warehouse No. 4 offers the above 'arrowheads' to the Winged Guard."

…Why can't we go in their place?

She knew.

Matured youth had incredibly strong firepower. The high-ranking officials in the Guard knew very well what it meant to fight at their expense. They were probably much more aware as they weren't at the whim of their sentiments, like herself.

Yet, they would never be able to defeat their attackers if they weren't truly prepared to eventually lose that firepower forever.

No one could replace them. What could a single cup of water do with a blazing fire that engulfed an entire island? Even if others feared her because she was a troll, in the end, Nygglatho was little more than that cup. She could not protect anything she wanted to keep safe. She could not take anything she wanted to whisk away.

She knew.

But. Still. She knew, and what good did that do?

The connection on the communication crystal clicked off.

Whatever it was that kept her emotions in check burst into a million pieces.

"Aaahhhh!"

Nygglatho howled.

"Why?! Why this?!"

She looked up at the ceiling, her emotions gushing forth in a wail.

That mechanized version of herself she had made in her mind? That sickening thing should have gone straight into the trash. Thrown in the shredder and turned to scrap.

"Why…? Whyyy…?"

Her whirlpool of emotions quickly dried up.

Her cries died out and became quiet sobs.

Large tears welled up in her eyes, plopping one by one onto her knees and dampening her skirt.

There was a time when she had resolved to be a strong woman.

So the girls here would comfortably seek out her help. So she could be a pillar for their spirits. So even if clumsily, she could be the mother these parentless children had never had. Or at least play the part.

She should have made up her mind that day. No matter what happened, she would never cry. It was the girls themselves who should have been truly uneasy and desperate to shed tears. So she had to take on the role of a shoulder to cry on. So no matter how impossible it felt, no matter how much she had to suppress her feelings, she had to support the girls with a smile.

How stupid was that?

That was impossible.

She felt so sad. So defeated.

She couldn't restrain her tears and sobs.

"Ohhh…hahhh…"

The failure of a strong woman wailed like a baby.

No one would comfort her. There wasn't anyone who would offer her a shoulder to cry on. That's why she didn't know when to stop crying.

"Pardon us, it's an emergency!"

"There you are, Nygglatho!"

"Th-th-th-there's trouble!"

*   *   *

It happened so suddenly. The door swung open so violently she thought it had broken, and three little faeries leaped in.

"Ahh!"

It was lucky she was facing the communication crystal with her back to the door. Her sobs withdrew in surprise, and the girls didn't have to see her tear-streaked face.

"H-hold on, you're supposed to knock before entering."

Her voice was shaky, so she objected quietly, her back still to them. But—

"There's no time for that. I said it's an emergency!"

"Come quickly, otherwise we'll be in real trouble!"

"We'll have a death on our hands if you don't hurry up!"

Death?

Oh, well, she knew about that.

She knew that Chtholly Nota Seniorious would die. But that wouldn't happen for another three days. Chtholly was fifteen; she was one of the oldest girls and acted like an adult even though she was still very much a child, and in fact a bit spoiled, even though she wasn't very good at fawning over others. And—

"Mr. Willem is going to die!"

Silence.

…What? Going to die? Who? Willem?

One by one, words trickled into her heart, paralyzed by tears.

After a few seconds—

"How on earth did that happen?!"

Her voice, still a bit nasal, came out in a shriek as she grabbed her nearby spice case…just kidding, her first aid kit…then flew out of the room.

Once This War Is Over
-starry road to tomorrow-

1. That Day Long, Long Ago

A long fight finally drew to a close.

The sun had set three times and risen three more.

Ocean water rushed in where sheer mountains had stood before the war, forming a large bay.

The flames of purgatory unleashed upon the trees showed no signs of abating, continuing to spread death and black ash.

Countless metal fragments were scattered about. If someone knowledgeable examined the scene closely, it would have been evident they were the remains of ruined talismans. The majority of the shards had once been a part of the Deflect charm, manufactured to the highest of standards at the Holy Empire Central Workshop. The fragmented clusters of bronze floating in the bay's waves were broken pieces of the Allay Terminal Disease charm, passed down within the West Garmando Sands Federation. The molten iron bubbling red among the trees had, just a few days earlier, been the secret of the Selenzrode School of Magic, the Protection of Fate charm.

It was a grand collection of the greatest of battle magic used by all mankind, gathered from quite literally all over the world.

They had all been spent and now littered the ground.

"—Man, you sure made this take a while."

The young man felt like he didn't have enough strength to move even a single finger.

He tossed away his broken sword and sat on a nearby rock.

"No one told me I had to do this much to win, sheesh."

"I should be the one saying that, young one."

The air shuddered at the bitter voice.

The old man's voice sounded like it echoed from the depths of the abyss.

"However…I shall acknowledge that you have had your own way thus far by straining that punitive life of yours."

"That doesn't make me happy. Your recognition isn't gonna grant me more time… Also, you're talking like normal, but aren't you supposed to be dead?"

"Indeed. Even I, with my physical form so thoroughly destroyed as it is, must steep this body into the hush of death for a hundred years. What communicates with you now is, simply put, my echoes."

"Oh, great. That's a relief."

Eleven Percival-series swords with seven ruinous spells, "sharpened" to a level of self-destruction. He had even forced himself to use the Braves' final sword techniques, which he had no right to activate.

If all that hadn't killed it, there was nothing more he could do.

"I say this as I fully accept it, but what a terrifying tale. You wield so much power alone, despite how powerless you are. It is truly, truly frightening. Had you used that power in the realm of man, it could have reduced two or three kingdoms to ash in a single night. But…of course, it seems it was not power without price."

The young man snorted.

Long, stringy clouds of mist floated around the young man.

As they slowly, slowly grew in number, they coiled around his body, as though trying to bind him.

"That is the magnitude of that spell. The reaction becomes a curse and torments the caster. Casting just one is more than enough to shatter a person's body, and it would not be surprising if your very soul disappeared, as well. To cast seven of them—you may be plagued by unspeakable agony."

"If it's gonna end with me dying, then it doesn't matter if I cast one or seven, and if I can't fight anymore, then it doesn't matter if it hurts or I'm in pain."

"...*That does not seem like sound logic.*"

"People have been telling me that for years, but hearing it from a real monster makes it feel a little different."

The voice cackled.

"*You cannot stand up to the gods without such measures, hmm?*"

"*—Our time of parting has come to pass. I shall slumber now for a hundred years.*"

"Hurry up and get outta here. At least let it be quiet when I die."

"*Very well. I can recognize that much as your right as the victor—*"

The voice faded, and along with the overpowering sensation that filled the air around the young man, it vanished into the wind.

"Hey, you dead yet?"

He called, and no response came.

There was a dry *creak* by the young man's feet.

He used all his strength to lift his head and look down and saw that his ankles and feet had turned into rough, chunky stone.

—The hell is this?

There was a chorus of quiet crackling noises, and the gray crept up along his body. To his knees. To his thighs. To his waist. Then farther up.

One after the other, the seven curses that should have cost him his life...intermingled elaborately, and after a series of mutual interferences, they manifested in a completely divergent form.

As his chest began to petrify, the young man smiled again.

"I had planned on going home, though. How on earth did this happen?"

He looked up at the sky, and he imparted to all those precious to him under that same sky words that would never reach them.

"Sorry, Lillia. Get home safely with the master.

"Sorry, Suowong. I want you to go along with all of Lillia's requests from now on.

"Emi, I…I didn't promise you anything. I think you'll be fine on your own, but, well, at least live on happy and healthy."

Then… Then…

As he uttered his last words, the young man's body was turning to stone with frightening speed.

There were too many he wanted to name. He had so little time left.

There wasn't much he could do about it. He sifted through all the names that came to mind until only one remained in his sieve.

"Almaria, I'm really sorry—"

The last name he chose was that of his daughter, unrelated to him by blood, who awaited him in an orphanage far away.

"—I don't think I'll be back to eat that butter cake."

At last, there was a quiet *ding*.

All that was left was a hunk of stone in the shape of a young man.

2. The One Who Should Not Be Alive

"What is this?"

That was the first thing Nygglatho said once she was finished treating him.

"What is wrong with your body?"

"Ha-ha-ha, I guess you could say I've gotten pretty rusty. I haven't held a sword in ages, so my body couldn't keep up."

"I don't need to hear your jokes. You should know very well what this means or, at the very least, what sort of situation you're in."

Nygglatho wore a serious expression, and on top of that, her eyes were bloodshot for some reason and her voice shaky. It didn't seem like he'd be able to blow this off with a joke.

"To put it frankly? You're in tatters. You have hairline fractures in almost all your bones, and they're not healing. You have several weakened tendons, and they haven't recovered. Almost half your internal organs aren't working properly. Meditative healing isn't my specialty, so I'm not entirely sure, but viewed from that angle, it's safe to say your internal flow of energy is a complete mess."

He thought she was probably right. Willem didn't know anything about that but was aware that his body was a wreck.

"I wouldn't even have to pull out a knife for the fibers in your meat, either. They're so full of tears, I could rip them apart with my teeth alone."

He wished she wouldn't say that with such a sad look on her face.

"And these aren't wounds from yesterday or today. They're all old. Does that mean you've been keeping them a secret all this time?"

"It's not really a secret."

"It's the same even if you act indifferent and keep quiet about it! How much did you have to exercise to walk and move like this…?" Nygglatho sighed deeply. "…These wounds are the aftereffect of turning into stone, aren't they?"

"It's more like the damage from the fight before that happened. Well, I was in a state where just being alive was a huge bonus. I'm not asking for much."

"That's no excuse for treating your life so lightly."

"Guess not."

He shrugged—well, he wanted to, but pain shot throughout his entire body when he tried, so he just smiled vaguely instead.

"Don't push yourself too hard."

Nygglatho gently placed her palm on his hand.

Reflexively, his heart beat faster.

"You'll lose your flavor."

He'd thought she was going to say something like that.

"Can I tell the children?"

"Sure. Like I said, it really wasn't a secret to begin with. If you feel like you have to, tell them as much as you need."

"All right. I'll be off, then. You stay here and rest in the meantime. I think you know this already, but anything that will put a strain on your body is absolutely forbidden, okay? I can't guarantee the life of someone clinging to it under such mysterious circumstances."

"Got it. I'm not gonna do anything that'll add an extra dish to your dinner," he strained to say.

"This is not funny. I'm being serious."

"…O-okay."

She huffed at him with a serious expression and pouted her lips, but it wasn't very intimidating.

Who was it who'd been talking about flavor just now? He felt like something was unfair about this, but he didn't protest.

That would probably be best for his health, but…more importantly, he knew it wasn't very good manners to use a joke to hide how embarrassed he was that someone was worried for him.

She chose the dining hall as the place for all the faeries to gather.

Nygglatho garnered the attention of almost twenty of them, then sighed.

"…I see you're all looking at me with such expectant faces, but it might not be a very fun story, okay?"

"Well, we can decide that afterward. We're, you know…not really excited, but we want to know the truth."

Ithea had spoken. The faeries around her nodded eagerly.

It didn't seem Nygglatho would be getting out of this one. "I suppose I have no choice," she muttered, readying herself, and began to speak.

"It was around spring last year, I think. Just before I was dispatched here. I had to work together with salvagers once, under orders of the Orlandry Alliance."

"Salvagers!!"

The eyes of several faeries glittered. The salvagers, chasers of romance who dove headfirst into danger, had a heroic popularity among some of the children in Regule Aire. That being said, they were rather more popular with boys.

"They were basically not very good at their jobs. They went down to the surface many times, but they didn't bring back much. That day, they were just about to return to the islands empty-handed, but a clumsy fellow stepped through the ground and fell in—"

There, the troupe had discovered an enormous frozen underground lake.

Then they'd spotted a stone statue of a young featureless man sunken at the bottom of the lake, she explained.

"It's like 'Icicle Coffin.'" One of the girls mentioned the title of a fairy tale.

"There wasn't a princess inside but a statue of a man."

One of their companions who could use Sight noticed that it wasn't just a statue but a real person turned into stone by some sort of curse. After that, of course, they'd lost the option of just going home and leaving him untouched.

They laboriously shattered the ice and pulled out the statue. It was a heavy load, but they managed to take it back to the island.

After throwing him in a charity hospital for about a month, the petrification finally wore off, and he woke up.

"It was quite the hassle, then. He would act unruly whenever he saw a boggard or an orc, and he couldn't understand our language at all. We brought in a communications master from the Alliance, and we were able to talk with him for the first time. Eventually, we found out that he was a real emnetwiht. The last surviving soldier of a race that had made enemies of everyone but themselves. I don't know why, but he slept for hundreds of years at the bottom of that lake…"

"He was on the surface that whole time and was never eaten by a Beast?"

"Possibly because he had turned to stone. Arguably the only good thing to come of the situation."

The language problem had been comparatively easy to solve. One of the ancient talismans on the ground near the ice was Language Comprehension. The young man used the charm and began talking about himself bit by bit, and he understood the information about the present the salvagers explained to him.

Nygglatho still remembered the expression of despair on his face.

She couldn't forget how he'd wailed in lament.

He was most likely the last of the emnetwiht, who should have all perished long ago. The companions decided to leave this special being alone, just as he wished.

Nygglatho didn't know much about what happened afterward. The man went on to live on Island No. 28 of all places—making his home where people were most critical of the featureless—and worked incredibly hard to pay off the debt he had incurred from the analeptics, the hospital, the communications master, etc. That was about as much as she heard from one of the salvagers.

Then…that's right. He'd come here.

The young man had grown in this past year and a half. His smile came out more now. He even showed how oddly nice he was toward the children.

And yet. The pitch-black flame of emptiness that gloomily shivered deep in his eyes had not changed from back then.

"That's all I know."

Withholding some of the more subjective things, Nygglatho finished telling the general story.

The girls looked at one another, whispering among themselves in some sort of exchange.

"—And that's all I can tell you. Another thing I can do is ask you a favor. It might not be possible right away, but please don't be too afraid of him or alienate him too much… That's all." With that, Nygglatho took her leave of the dining hall.

As Nygglatho walked down the corridor, she thought to herself, *I think I made a mistake.*

The emnetwiht race was detested. Willem himself might not have had anything to do with it, but it had been, without a doubt, the emnetwiht who'd unleashed the Seventeen Beasts to begin destroying the world.

She didn't think these leprechauns would treat him the same as the rest of society. But even if they didn't act that way, it was possible they would respond similarly. The girls were beings meant to fight against the Seventeen Beasts, weapons that were exhausted in those battles. The responsibility for creating this fate of theirs, if they traced it all the way back, lay with the emnetwiht.

And yet. If it was something she could prevent—she didn't want the kids to reject him.

She didn't want to destroy this place, where that young man somehow managed a smile despite the fact that there was no home for him left in this world.

Nygglatho was sure he didn't wish for something like that. He'd tried to learn the truth about the faeries and had revealed the truth about himself. Nygglatho didn't want his decisions to go to waste. That was why she brought up the past. Still, that didn't mean her desire not to give up had disappeared.

She knew how selfish it was, but somehow, she wanted the children to stay by Willem's side, as they always had—

She stopped in her tracks.

An uneasy sensation tickled the back of her neck.

No.

Such a thing couldn't be happening now, not with this timing. But at the same time, she also thought it was something they'd do.

Quickly, about-face. She rushed toward the infirmary.

Just as she approached the corner in the corridor—

"Willie! We heard the story! You were destroyed?"

She heard carefree voices.

She stumbled forward.

"Wow, emnetwiht are a lot like us!"

"Very interesting. I hope you'll tell us stories about your time."

"U-um, I don't know how to say this very well, but please cheer up."

The infirmary was crowded with faeries.

They were crowded around the bed of a patient with serious injuries who'd been on the verge of death just moments earlier, and they were making quite a ruckus.

"..."

Nygglatho stood absently in front of the door for about ten seconds.

Another five seconds to smile at how ridiculous her worries had been. Honestly, she could have easily imagined things ending up this way; what had she been so afraid of?

She was so happy to see the girls all trying to encourage Willem each in her own way and took another two seconds to wipe the smile off her face.

A full seven seconds to take a deep breath and switch modes.

"Girls?"

The lot of them froze in place.

With the creaky sound of a rusty screw, they all turned their heads to look at her.

"The patient is very tired right now and is resting. You need to be quiet. Bad children that don't listen..."

Slowly, calmly, a smile spread across her face like a tear in fabric.

"...know what happens to them, don't they?"

It didn't even take ten seconds. The girls pushed out of the room and sprinted down the hall.

"Wow, sure is quiet now." Ithea peeked out from behind her.

"If you're going to be noisy, then I'll chase you away, too."

"Nya-ha-ha, I'd prefer you didn't." She smiled lightly, a vague expression on her face making it difficult to tell if she was serious or joking. "But there's something I want to check with the dying man here. You think you can let me do that?"

"...What do you want to ask?"

Before Nygglatho could say anything, Willem responded.

Nygglatho wouldn't be able to interject now. "Thanks," Ithea said with her usual smile, slipping into the room and sitting down in a small chair situated by the side of the bed.

"First, let me just reconfirm: You're emnetwiht, right?"

"I guess at some point, we started being called that. When I lived on the surface, we didn't go out of our way to give our race a special name. We were just people, and any other race was treated as a monstrosity."

"Barbarous times, they were."

"Well, I won't deny that... So what are you getting at?"

Ithea smiled complacently.

"...So why would such a great emnetwiht bother with us?" she asked, her expression suddenly growing serious, her voice low. "We're grateful for you, Second Enchantments Officer. But after hearing what you really are, I'm completely lost again as to why you'd use up all your energy in a place like this. Fighting with Chtholly when you're in such a tattered state just puts your life at risk. It's kind of weird that you'd do that much without a real reason, y'know?"

"Of course I want to be nice to girls."

"...That's a little straightforward." Ithea's expression softened, and she scratched her cheek with the tip of her finger. "Sure, biologists say it's natural for a male of a species to be kind toward its female counterparts, but I think you know, right? This is just appearance for us."

Leprechauns were all female.

She didn't know why, but it was a truth she couldn't do anything about. At the very least, she hadn't found any exceptions.

Strictly speaking, they weren't life-forms, but "things" that multiplied naturally, so there was no inherent liability to not having males. Therefore, no one thought it was much of a problem, but to put it another way:

"All of us are girls, so it's like we don't have a sex in the first place. We're basically slugs."

"I don't get it." Willem snorted with a smile. "The molding unit at the Capital Puppeteering Troupe would get so mad if they heard that."

"Huh? Sure, I guess, but I don't know who that is."

"...Then, I guess, it's like this. You like kittens?"

"Huh? Well, I guess as much as anyone else."

"You want to keep them safe?"

"Sure, as much as anyone else."

"That's basically it."

"Wait...I don't get what you mean."

Willem thought for a moment.

"This is something I heard long ago. Things that have adorable outward appearances don't just spring up randomly. They have an innate nature that wants to be loved, protected, cherished, so they develop that way.

"So whether animal or person, that's why kids are cute, regardless of race. They desperately hope that they're something people want to protect...understand?"

"...Are you saying we're the same?"

"You're irregular beings. Your origins are souls that could take on whatever aberrant form they wanted, but instead, you're born not only as children but as little girls. Does that convince you?"

"So you're a big ol' softy to your whole race, huh—? When we take into account your taste in young girls, Officer, then it all makes sense."

"Hey, come on, where'd you get that from?!"

The two laughed together.

What was that? Nygglatho wondered.

She felt miserable, fretting over what it was that made her worry so much.

In the end, neither the faeries nor Willem himself had considered what she'd been concerned about earlier as deeply as Nygglatho had expected; it was terribly egocentric of her. Everyone only ever acted according to their own logic and standards.

To put it simply, they were just a herd of idiots.

And idiots were idiots because they couldn't become sharp that quickly.

They were idiots because they could laugh so freely.

Ohhh, I love you all so much.

For some reason, everyone got incredibly frightened when she said things like that out loud, so she settled on yelling it in her heart.

3. The Stray Girl and the Flying Lizard

...What am I doing?

Chtholly Nota Seniorious ran. She flew from her living quarters known as the warehouse, ran through the forest, ran through the port, and with no more land to run on, she sprouted wings from her back and flew.

She didn't know why. But she had to.

She mostly understood what Willem had wanted to convey through that (what Chtholly considered) sham fight. That had been a mistake. And she couldn't handle it.

Comparing the current Guard's deployable firepower and the strength of the group to Timere, whose attack was imminent, it was impossible to guarantee victory. That was why she had to be ready to be a sacrifice in order to temporarily raise the bar on their power. That was the current situation.

But there was another solution: Raise the standard of firepower itself.

They'd known all along that they were not using the dug weapons to their fullest potential. They were complicated creations made so long ago, after all, and even if they weren't, their capabilities had naturally deteriorated. Not only that, but none of them came with an instruction manual, so the users had to feel out how to activate them by trial and error, bypassing the user authentication with dummies—in other words, using faeries to get by. For all their efforts, they just barely managed to force the weapons to activate.

It was obvious. Once someone who knew how they were meant to be used showed up, the whole situation changed.

It was time to reevaluate their forces. They could once again place their two choices on the scales: "Victory at the expense of countless lives" and "Certain victory with the least amount of sacrifices."

*   *   *

It would be the same as recognizing their fights had been misguided up to that point.

It would be the same as rubbing their noses in the fact that everyone they had lost until now had been no more than pointless victims.

It would be the same as determining her resolve, as someone prepared for her own death and fully aware that she would be lost along the way just like all who'd gone before her, was in itself worthless.

"This isn't…funny…"

Six months ago.

The day they'd predicted an attack by an especially large Timere.

The moment they'd announced they had no other recourse but to push the leprechaun Chtholly Nota Seniorious into overdrive.

"But I was so scared…"

Of course she didn't want to die.

Once she knew her time was limited, she'd started thinking of things she wanted to do.

Even so, she'd cried and cried, putting on a strong face day after day.

"I was finally ready…"

Not even a month ago, she'd decided she wouldn't cry anymore, but now, she couldn't help the tears clouding her eyes.

No, I'm not gonna cry now. The more she forced herself, the less she could hold back the welling tears on the brink of spilling over.

"Gh, nghhh…!"

She squeezed her eyes shut. She stopped flapping her wings.

Her flight turned into a free fall. The wind howled in her ears.

Below her was a thick sea of white clouds.

Perfect, she thought.

She'd get soaked if she flew through the clouds. Then no one would be able to tell she'd been crying. She simply let her body drop.

Chtholly entered the clouds.

Clouds are essentially thick fog in high places. Though they looked like cotton, they felt like nothing, and though she had dived in, she didn't make a splash. What was there was simply a whiteness that filled her vision and a dampness—a void of nothingness in the sky.

"Oh—"

—*no*, she thought.

She'd forgotten a crucial detail.

It was autumn. Winter was nearing.

Once her whole body was wet, it became terribly cold.

"Shoot…"

Whether bird or faerie, physical strength is incredibly important during flight. The cold was rapidly stealing her strength. Even more alarming, there were no conveniently placed floating stones for her to rest on.

Should she fly to the nearest island?

Or just go back the way she came?

Neither were totally impossible. But when she thought about getting home, the former wasn't very realistic. Then, of course, she had no other option but to go the way she came, but she genuinely hesitated to act.

What should she do?

Her body shivered, falling backward through the clouds, and she weighed her choices. Though there was only one conclusion, she forced the conflict brewing inside her, as though she didn't want to do it.

While that was happening—

"Hmm…?"

—a black shadow suddenly emerged in a corner of her whitened vision.

Five minutes later.

The Winged Guard patrol airship *Barocupot*, inside the small war room on the second deck.

It was cramped.

Incredibly cramped.

It was, of course, the small war room and consequently not very big.

However, it was a war room and had to be large enough to fit a certain number of people. There were only two occupants now.

So why did she feel so cramped?

The answer was simple. One of the two was a giant lizardfolk, easily twice Chtholly's height. Double her height meant double her weight, and his intensity was eight times as great. The room felt much smaller.

After she scrubbed her head with a borrowed towel, Chtholly looked up at the lizardfolk's face.

"...I'm sorry for intruding so suddenly, First Officer Limeskin. I saw you flying nearby, I just..."

"I do not mind. The hermitage of wind is alwaysss open to the warrior," the lizardfolk said as he placed a warm cup of medicinal tea onto the table.

There was a surreal humor in the way he hunched over, gently holding the small cup like a toy.

"Thank you."

She took the cup and brought it to her lips.

It was hot. And bitter. Her body involuntarily stiffened as a prickly sensation tickled the tip of her tongue.

"However, I do wonder whhhy you were flying through the cloudss in thisss ssseasson. Not to mention, you have a very important fight before you. What happened?"

"Urgh..."

She faltered.

She hesitated. She wavered. She thought. Then she opened her mouth.

"About that fight... It would be bad to say that I am afraid of dying just before it, wouldn't it?"

"Hmm?"

The lizardfolk raised an eyebrow, or so it looked. He, of course, didn't have eyebrows, so it was just her imagination.

"It's...Willem, Second Enchantments Officer Willem."

"Hmm."

Chtholly knew. Second Enchantments Officer Willem Kmetsch currently stationed at the faerie warehouse was a soldier who only existed on paper, nothing but a rank. But nonetheless, he was a soldier who definitely existed in military documents. And his direct superior on paper was the giant lizardfolk that sat before her—First Officer Limeskin.

"He said he has a different way of fighting than the one we've always used. He actually showed me a bit of it. I couldn't make out what he did very well, but it made me understand something very clearly. It would certainly have a higher chance of victory, be more effective, and…is much more correct than our way."

"Oh…?"

She dropped her gaze into the cup.

"I don't want to accept this. I don't want to believe that all my sisters before me were wrong and didn't have to die. That was why I wasn't going to listen to him. I didn't have any time left anyhow. I was going to prove it on the battlefield. I thought I had to protect the way my sisters fought, to prove that they were right. But…"

"Were you afraid?"

She couldn't nod straightaway.

Limeskin was very particular about the word *warrior*. Perhaps it was characteristic of the lizardfolk race. Chtholly didn't understand the details of his strict definition, but apparently, she was recognized as a warrior in accordance with his own standards.

If she nodded now, he would probably be disappointed in her.

He might see it as her losing courage and throwing away her qualifications to be a warrior.

But even so…

"…Yes."

She could not lie.

"*Kh-kh-kh*, I sssee."

Suddenly—

The lizardfolk opened his mouth wide. The rasping clang that sounded like a ceramic bell being whirled about surged from the depths of his throat.

"…Huh? Huh?"

An odd, loud voice reverberated far above her head.

"I sssee. Thiss meanss we musst apologizze to the man. Though hiss battlefield differesss from oursss, he iss undoubtedly a warrior himssself."

It took her a while to realize he was laughing.

"Wh-why? Why do you think that? We're the ones fighting!"

"To fight againsst the Beasstsss is our war. But that iss not Willem'ss war. What he iss trying to contend with iss the wind inssside of you."

"…The wind?"

"The identity of what you call 'ressolve.' Perhapsss it is eassier to undersssstand if I call it 'resssignation'?"

Blood rushed to her head.

She drank down the entire cup of medicinal tea. Her insides grew hot as though she was being roasted.

What on earth do they boil to make something like this? Why would the cold-blooded lizardfolk make something like this anyway? Several absurd questions came to mind, but Chtholly shoved them all into the corner of her thoughts. Now was not the time to be dwelling on such things.

"Why—?"

Her heart felt lighter. It also felt like a hole had opened inside it, but that probably didn't make much of a difference.

"First Officer, you knew I never had the qualifications to be a warrior, didn't you? You are quite adept at flattery, after all… I was being quite serious."

"What are you talking about? Like the ssun sssetting in the north, it iss unthinkable for the proud ssscaled people to sspeak liesss."

"But didn't you just say I was resigned?"

"Resssignation and resssolve are, in essence, the sssame thing. Both indicate the abandonment of sssomething important for the ssake of one'sss goalss."

—*That's…*

That line of thinking jumbled the sacred and the abominable into one.

"Isn't resolve supposed to be, like, something much more important?"

"The value of everything iss determined only by the weight of the

cossst. There iss worth in the ressolve of throwing away what iss important. And naturally, the resssignation of doing the same iss worth jussst asss
much."

"I don't really understand."

"Cssertainly, I cannot ssay it iss not befitting of a warrior to be con-
founded by the beauty of wordsss," he said, his unearthly laugh rattling in
his throat.

"Then…what should I do?"

"That iss up to you."

"…I'm asking because I don't know. What is the right answer?"

"There iss no sssuch fanciful thing asss a 'right ansssswer' on the battlefield. That iss why the warrior musst embrace the wind that blowsss within
her. Ssso that she may be led along on a guidelessss road."

"…First Officer…"

Oh no.

She had no idea what he was earnestly trying to say.

She'd understood everything until a few moments ago. Regardless of
whether she was happy with his insight, she'd managed to grasp what he
was trying to convey. But likely since he had grown more invested in the
subject, his circular way of talking and the details of the conversation itself
were growing more and more complicated.

She felt like he was saying something important to her, and it wasn't
something that totally escaped her emotional grasp, but she had no idea
what he meant.

"You ssaid you wisshed to protect the righteousssnesss of your ssissterss'
fight, yesss?"

"…Yes."

"Then, before the fight, I want you to disscover what that righteoussss-
ness iss. We only understand your fight intellectually. The work itssself,
your hissstory, the emotional hisstory that hidesss behind it—everything.
Ssso it iss only you who hasss the right to evaluate what iss righteouss."

"…That's irresponsible of you, First Officer."

"The wind blowsss unburdened."

He brushed it off with (what looked like) a cool expression.

Chtholly sighed slightly. For some reason, she now felt like giving up on a lot of things.

Right, hadn't she just been told that resignation and resolve were the same thing? Now that made sense. Now that she thought about it, she certainly felt like she had guts.

"…You might get angry at me, but I need to tell you something."

"What?"

"I actually never wanted to be a warrior."

His throat rattled in a cackle.

"I know. That iss why you have become a sssplendid warrior."

…They really weren't on the same page.

Damn it all…

She swallowed her frustration as she gulped down her second cup of medicinal tea.

4. The Starry Sky Beneath the Starry Sky

"She's currently aboard a Winged Guard patrol airship near Island No. 66."

"…How'd that happen?"

"I don't know, but they told me she was coming back now. They said they would take her part of the way and that she would make the rest of the trip on foot."

Nygglatho clicked off the connection on the communication crystal.

"Sure was an interesting way to run away from home, huh? Worried me sick."

"I know—I'm so envious of the children with wings. They have such an abundance of ways to express themselves. All I can do to relieve my stress when I'm upset is binge eat." She sighed, a hint of sorrow in her expression. "They really do adore you. Not only her, but the others as well. I'm a bit jealous, I suppose, as their caretaker."

"Yeah? Like how?"

"Oh, have you not noticed?" Nygglatho placed a hand to her mouth with a look of surprise. "Are you the dull sort? Or are you simply good at hiding it?"

"The hell do you mean?"

"Let's see. There is a broad group of awful men who insist they have no interest in romance but actually want girls to approach them and feel good."

...What does that *mean?*

"The dull ones actually don't notice when someone likes them and never do, no matter what happens. It's rather enjoyable to see the girl's impatience after nothing she says or does works and the interesting ways her attempts escalate. In another variation, there are the mistaken sort of men who confuse the affection the girl shows him for a different feeling.

"The ones who hide it actually realize when someone likes them, but they purposefully act like they don't. They're similar to the dull ones but have the characteristic of adding plenty of spice, like feelings of guilt for tricking the other or situations where the smitten ends up realizing he's pretending not to notice.

"So which are you?"

"...This is ridiculous. I don't even know what I should call bullshit on first." Willem sighed deeply. "Take your fiction somewhere else. I'm not gonna deny they act like they're interested in me or anything like that."

"Oh." Nygglatho's eyes widened. "That was unexpected. Almost as though you plan to go with the disinterested act."

"Don't call it an act. I'm not putting on a show here." He scratched his head. "I'm being serious now. Romantic feelings just bubble up from within by themselves when you get old enough, whether you have someone or not. Most people just find someone close at hand to throw their feelings at, whether that's someone of the opposite sex who happens to be nearby, or a person they look up to who's out of reach, or even an ideal they might find one day out in the world. In some cases, they channel their feelings and everything at a daydream that doesn't exist... But those girls have never been able to do any of that.

"Then I come in. I took things that were at zero and turned them into one. Now they suddenly have somewhere to direct their feelings. If they can give a good excuse for those feelings they've got bottled up, that means they've created an excellent romance for themselves— What's with the stare?"

A sharp glare of disgust bored straight through Willem.

"It's a look of astonishment at having found a man far more awful than I'd imagined."

"Why? It's normal. To be blunt, most girls end up with a strong father complex at one point or another. The fact they like me makes me happy, and it's an honor, but there's nothing more to it."

"...That was an incredibly underwhelming answer."

Nygglatho's tone was clearly dissatisfied, so he just shrugged.

"Underwhelming just means things are quiet. Isn't that a good thing?"

"Well... Yes, I won't deny that. But"—Nygglatho pointed straight at his chest—"let me say this as a girl myself: It is absolutely unbearable to have your feelings ignored so philosophically. The kids might certainly be children, but they are girls. I can't stand men who refuse to recognize that. I'm sure they're terrible for my digestion."

As a girl, huh? I'm not sure she's young enough to call herself that.

No, he wouldn't dare touch that. He was a considerate enough man to do that much. He didn't want to be digested.

"...No matter how young those feelings might be, too. For some of the children, those are their last thoughts, so I want you to confront those emotions properly. No more jokes. I ask you this earnestly, from the bottom of my heart."

"No."

Willem's response was curt.

"...If love and romance are supposed to be so wonderful, then how is a temporary fling in a tiny place like this supposed to help? Regule Aire is huge. There's a handful of other amazing men. Acting and working as a father means having your daughters snatched up by one of those guys one day," he insisted.

Willem had never looked at his surroundings with that in mind, so all the guys he knew on Regule Aire had green skin or pigs' faces or were covered in scales.

No, wait. Maybe a preoccupation with appearances and differences in races was a sensibility five hundred years outdated. In fact, there were plenty of good guys if he went by personality alone.

To test himself, he imagined a scenario.

One day, Chtholly, for example, suddenly announces, "*I am in a serious relationship*," and brings home a nice young boggard. Could he bless them with a smile in the end if that happened?

"Gyah?!"

"…Oh, I'm sorry. Felt just a little bloodthirsty there."

"Th-that wasn't just 'a little'!! I just saw my grandmother beckoning me from beyond the River of the Dead!! What in the world was that?!"

"Well, I was just thinking how Glick and those guys don't look it but are actually good guys, and I just, y'know."

"There's a limit to how incoherent you can be, you know!!"

He suddenly turned to look out the window.

It was a nice, clear night.

"I'm going out. If you have anything more to say, save it for later."

"Hey, where are you going?"

"Probably look at the stars. Oh, and I'm taking this key with me."

He waved his hand lazily and left the room.

"Huh? What? Wait, how did you—?!"

He pretended not to hear the screams behind him.

He pulled Seniorious out of storage.

There was a small hill on the outskirts of Island No. 68.

The wind was calm, the air was clear, and the light from the stars soft. It was a convenient night.

Willem pulled off the cloth covering Seniorious and exposed the blade to the wind.

He let a bit of venenum flow into it. His temples ached slightly but not enough to worry over.

Fwoom. Seniorious emitted a soft light.

"—Initialize adjustment."

He murmured and touched one of the metal fragments near the center. There was a quiet *thunk*. The fragment parted from the blade on its own, glided across the air, and stopped in place about five paces from Willem.

There came a clear metallic sound, like a metallophone being struck.

He touched another piece. That, too, glided across the air and stopped a ways away. A clear sound echoed in a pitch slightly different from the one before it.

Another one.

And another one.

The most ancient holy sword of Seniorious was comprised of a total of forty-one pieces and held together by veins of enchantment. By directly manipulating those veins, he could take the blade apart like this and expose each component individually.

Finally, all that was left near Willem was a small fragment of crystal which had been hidden inside the blade.

Surrounding it were forty-one fragments emitting faint, starlike light.

"All right…"

He brushed his hand against the crystal and began assessing what sort of state Seniorious was in.

Its anti-poison and anti-curse resistance effects were higher than normal. On the other hand, its anti-confusion and anti-dragonsight effects had almost completely worn out. It also worried him how high the anti-demirace slayer levels were. This all must have been due to how long it'd been fighting without adjustment, influenced by battlefield stimuli and the users' habits.

Next, he checked every parameter.

It was actually in terrible shape. Due to how long they'd been han-dling it by forcing venenum through the hilt, all sorts of functions were out of order. There was a large venenum blockage in the spinal root—five knots of all sizes on either side. Three of the veins around that area had been completely cut off, and the rest of the veins themselves had become impaired and, on average, 30 percent less effective.

"You've done well, too, fighting like this all this time."

A bitter laugh escaped his lips.

He lightly struck the crystal with the tip of his finger. He sent off a bit of venenum into it.

The venenum lit a vein that had been invisible before, and it pulled in one of the metal fragments. Again came the metallic sound.

He sent off a different sort of venenum. A different vein glowed, and a different fragment played a note.

Another.

And another.

The lights danced one after the other. The sound leaped together.

The once sleeping veins of enchantment had been reinforced. The exhausted metal fragments filled with energy again.

—Willem felt a presence behind him.

"Hey. Welcome back, runaway," he called out without bothering to turn around.

"...What...are you doing?"

Without any sort of greeting, the intruder at his rear reprimanded him.

"Can't you tell? Maintenance for your partner."

"Hey. You can't just do this without permission from its compatible user."

"It's my responsibility to manage the place. Giving myself permission should be enough."

He cackled.

"That laugh doesn't suit you."

"Hmm, you think?"

"I like that softer laugh you always make better."

"Hmm...I—I see."

Willem had mentioned that he was aware the girls adored him.

He had simply snubbed their feelings with rationalization, acting like he didn't really care.

And yet, in just that moment, his heart skipped a beat.

"Come on. Keep playing."

"Playing?"

"You were making some nice music, weren't you? The melody was all over the place, though."

"I wasn't performing or anything."

"Then just busk. I don't have any money, though."

"...Man, I've got a weird audience now."

He returned his attention to the nearby crystal.

Chtholly sat behind Willem, her back facing his.

Gooong, gooong—the clear sound once again echoed through the night-time hills.

"What is this light?"

"Each Carillon is like a little microcosm, made up of a collection of many kinds of talismans, tied together with veins of enchantment, and sealed into the shape of a sword. You know what talismans are, right?"

"I've heard of them."

In the current era, talismans were considered curios and ancient treasures, the detailed manufacturing methods having been lost.

They were powerful effects of spells and talents engraved onto small pieces of paper, ceramic, or even metal. Those holding those pieces of paper or ceramic or metal benefited from the spell engraved on that small thing.

Even now, they were salvaged from the surface once in a while, and so they commonly circulated within the wealthier circles in Regule Aire.

"The one floating in front of you is a talisman to keep your tongue from burning when you drink something hot."

"...Huh?"

"Beside it is one for knowing which way is north in a place you visit for the first time. The one above that prevents nightmares while you're sick. And then from there, there's one to make you good at imitating a cat's meow, one to make sure you don't cut your nails too closely with a blade without venenum, and one to make heads appear sixty percent of the time when you flip a coin."

"Wait, hold on. This is Seniorious, right? The legendary weapon? Not a top hundred list of the greatest good luck items, right?"

"It happens with food sometimes. There are some combinations where, if eaten separately, they're fine, but if you eat them all one after the other, they'll make you sick. This was made along the same line of thought. Put talismans in a bunch and thread them together with veins of enchantment, then after complicated, mysterious interactions with one another, they start producing completely different effects. I don't know the details since I'm not a specialist, but that's what the guys at the Central Workshop said.

"Seniorious, especially, is one of the very oldest Carillons. Unlike the ones produced later at the workshop, I heard it was born on the battlefield as a result of a miraculous coincidence. That's why it uses so many talismans that just seem like makeshift parts."

"...Uh-huh..." Chtholly whipped her head around, looking at all forty-one talismans, forty-one small wishes. "I didn't know that. It's a legendary holy sword, so I thought it was brought into existence as a gift from the gods or something like that."

"Yeah, it's too bad."

The emnetwiht at the time needed them to survive. They used anything they could to accomplish that. War was an ugly reality. And yet, they yearned for beauty...

That's why they called the symbol of the power they finally achieved the Carillon—the holy swords.

"I see. I get it."

The girl fell silent.

He continued working. The metallic lights and sounds gently enveloped the silent pair.

"I just had a talk with the first officer before this," Chtholly said quietly, beginning her monologue. "He said that if I didn't feel like it before the day comes, then I don't have to open the gates to the faerie home. He said I could risk the fate of Island No. 15 based on the potential of my resolve and strength."

"…I see."

"Could I really get stronger?"

"I will make you stronger, even if you don't want to. That's my responsibility as a manager."

"That's what I thought you'd say." Her back twitched in a chuckle. "Then I shall take you up on your kind offer and tell you something. I doooon't wanna get any stronger!"

"Wait. Isn't this the part where you're supposed to realize you've been so surrounded by love all this time and start being honest with your feelings while breaking into tears?"

"…I am being honest. Realize that, idiot."

He pretended not to hear her muttering.

Now he saw how he'd become the kind of guy he'd heard about earlier, one who'd "hide it." The feeling of guilt was way worse than he'd initially imagined.

"—Right. Then how about if you come back alive from the fight, I promise to grant you one request. Let's start with that."

"Huh?" For a second, she gave a shocked response. "I…I don't really want you to do anything for me. And I mean, you say *anything*, but I know you won't do anything major. Like, if I told you to marry me—"

"No thanks."

He interrupted, cutting her short.

"…I'm not disappointed or anything, but I just want to hear your reasons. Why?"

"'Cause it's just not in the realm of possibility for me. Like it would be impossible if you asked me to bring back the dead or wipe out all the Beasts."

"What? You're saying that's on the same level as all of those things?"

"Sure is."

It was normal for children of a certain age to grow infatuated with an older, reliable member of the opposite sex close by.

It certainly might qualify as a sort of romance, but it was also like a temporary fever, brought on by a lack of options.

Therefore, it was also the natural duty of the adult to put some distance between them and watch over the child until that fever died down.

"At the very least, y'know, try again when you've grown up a bit."

"This wouldn't be so hard if I had—!"

Time—he cut off what would have been her last word.

"You do have time."

Chtholly gulped.

"That's something you will fight to earn. Right?"

"…I don't know if it'll work out like that."

"That's why you head out with a reason why you can't die, so you can know. Know what I mean? You might complain, but I heard that soldiers with fiancées waiting for them at home had higher survival rates. I've honestly seen some guys with enough spirit to keep living by drinking mud."

"My chance to have a fiancé was just shattered a couple of seconds ago, though."

He could feel her clammy stare.

"Oh, well, you know. You can't go for it if it's a future that's too unrealistic. I'm saying you need to find yourself a dream that's more grounded."

"I think what you're saying is outrageous. If you're trying to make me fight for an ideal, then you can't make me think about reality."

"…That was smart."

Willem could only manage a dry laugh.

Head out with a reason why you can't die—of course, those weren't Willem's words.

He was just borrowing someone else's, and after he'd been told that, he'd ended up resorting to a suicide attack, never returning to the place he was meant to. Though she probably hadn't seen through all of that, she'd noticed how shallow his words were or something to that effect.

"I'm smart, so stop treating me like a child."

"Nah, I can't."

"Why is it that's the only thing you're so stubborn about? Sheesh."

In a strangely mature manner, Chtholly exhaled.

"…Sweets."

"Hmm?"

"You made something in the dining hall several days ago. Do you know any other recipes?"

"Oh, well, several."

"Then can you make butter cake?"

Hah.

"Of all things, huh?"

"Huh?"

"Nope, it's nothing."

It wasn't that he hadn't expected it.

He sort of felt like that was where the conversation was headed.

"I know how to make it. My master forced me to learn. Someone close by could make it way better than me, though, so I've never really baked it myself."

"As long as you can make it, that's fine. Whenever one of the older girls came home from a fight, she would always wolf down and savor the butter cake. But by the time I was old enough to hold a sword, it was already off the dessert menu, and I could never do the same. So please."

He inhaled deeply.

He held his breath, then exhaled.

"Guess I don't have much of a choice."

Willem resumed the work at hand.

He finished adjusting Seniorious. He reset all the resistance levels, leaving only curse resistance slightly higher. It was probably a safe enough guess that Chtholly wouldn't be fighting other demiraces, so he reset all the slayer levels to default. By doing so, the stabilization of basic functions spread throughout all the veins capable of taking it.

He flicked the crystal fragment with the tip of his finger.

The metal pieces that floated around them glided through the air, one by one, gathering around the crystal.

When one returned to its original spot, a quiet strum echoed.

Once the short performance was over, the single large blade had finally regained its shape. The heavy weight was profound in Willem's hands.

"All right, all right. Okay. I'll make you eat so much cake, you'll get heartburn. You understand, yeah? So you have to come back."

He handed Seniorious over to the correct false owner.

"Leave it to me," the girl said and smiled.

5. Even When That War Ends

They wore informal armor over their military uniforms. Awkwardly large swords had been strapped to their backs.

All three girls were finished preparing for battle.

"All righty, then, we'll be back!" Ithea waved with her usual smile.

"…Mm." Nephren nodded slightly.

It was only Chtholly who did not turn back. She didn't say anything. The silver brooch on her uniform breast glinted dully, as though speaking.

And so the three faeries flew off.

Their figures melted into the sunset.

"…Dude, are you an idiot?!"

That was the first thing Glick said after hearing the story.

"Why'd you come all the way here? Just to eat with me?!"

"Why? I just told you. I'm giving you my status report and my thanks."

"You could do that literally any other time! Don't you understand that now is called now because now only exists now?!"

"...I mean, do *you* even understand what you're saying?"

"I don't care about me! We're talking about you! YOU!!"

Well, that was true.

Slightly perplexed by his boggard friend's unexpected indignation, Willem tilted his cup of salty coffee.

"My head's already full knowing there've been victims and drama behind Regule Aire's shadow of peace, damn it. I mean, even if I didn't know, it's the Guard's job to spill blood, and the more I think about it, it should be a given, but imagining it and actually hearing about it are way different. I feel like I'm gonna be crushed by the sinfulness of not knowing, and I want to go give those kids a hug right now—and what is up with that scary face of yours?"

"Nothing."

While on the receiving end of a fierce look that would certainly bring timid children to tears, Willem emptied his cup.

Glick heaved a heavy sigh.

"I heard it was light and easy work, so I offered it to you. Whether that was a good idea or not in the end, just thinking about what would've happened if I hadn't thought much of it and just gave it to some other guy makes me scared." He threw back his coffee. "...And. Why are you here?"

"Dunno what to say, but they're fighting tomorrow on Island No. 15 and will be for days. We're not gonna get any correspondence until much later. There's not a lot I can do right now."

"That's not what I mean! This is usually the part where you're so worried your food won't go down your throat and you can't sleep at night! So why are you so set on passing time like nothing's happening?!"

"Worrying about it now isn't gonna change their chances of victory. I've told them all I could up till yesterday, and I've adjusted their swords best I could. But still, their chances of safely winning is only a little more than half. If I let myself start worrying, I don't think my body could handle it."

"Come on, something's wrong here. You're not supposed to doubt their victory!"

"It goes against my principles to look away from reality."

"I'm saying, you're not supposed to look away from hope and dreams! A believing heart might have some mysterious power, y'know!"

"Everyone struggles because it doesn't. You can't return to reality when something unexpected happens if you desperately convince yourself it does. I need to be able to accept whatever happens to them, especially since I do believe in them."

"You wet blanket! Where's the fiery passion in your words?!"

"Guess I'm not the kind of person meant for a life of salvaging." Willem cackled and stood from his seat.

"What? You got something to do?"

"Yeah, just need to pick up some ingredients."

"Come on… You really serious about living life like nothing's going on?"

"Absolutely. There are girls out there fighting for this life."

Glick fell silent.

With a word of parting, Willem rose from his chair, but "…Oh, right." He recalled he had one thing to ask and stopped.

"Hey. You know where I can get butter and flour for cheap around here?"

✝

Then, Willem returned to Orlandry Alliance Warehouse No. 4.

"Willie!!"

The girls, who had been chasing a ball in the field, noticed him and all trotted over.

"Where were you? We were looking for you."

"Um, um, would you mind playing with us? It's been a while."

"We haven't heard from you lately, since you've been injured and what-not. So I won't punish you if you play with us today."

They tugged on his sleeves. But—

"Sorry. I've got something I need to do today."

"Awww," came cries of objection.

"Next time."

Leaving the complaints behind him, he headed straight for the kitchen.

He flipped through all the recipes for easy desserts popular with small children in his head. He found the page for butter cake.

He'd never managed this successfully at the orphanage (since his attempts were always compared to his daughter's), so the details were fuzzy. But he'd manage somehow. He had time to practice. And he was sure that just a tablespoon of love could change the flavor drastically.

"————————D————————a————————d————————"

Suddenly.

From somewhere.

He thought he heard a voice.

"…Almaria?"

He turned around, looked up at the sky. Of course, no one was there. Beyond the crimson-and-vermilion gradient spread of silklike clouds…

The owner of that voice no longer existed in this world.

She'd left without ever welcoming home the one for whom she'd been waiting, waiting and baking butter cakes at the orphanage. He never returned.

"I'm sorry."

He felt like he was doing something terrible.

It wasn't just to Almaria. He apologized to the companions he'd fought alongside then, too. And to the members of the royal family who'd seen them off with such high expectations.

Why couldn't he have died with her and the others? Moreover, why hadn't he ended his life as soon as he woke up in this world? Wasn't living as he was now betraying all the promises he'd once made?

And yet. He knew all of this, but now—

"I'm so, so sorry."

He bowed his head to the heavens.

There was no home for him in this world.

But if there was someone out there who would be his home…

Then he would stay so they could welcome him back.

His decision settling in his heart, he reached for his apron.

Before This World Ends——B
-promise/result-

In the dark of night.

A lone Beast howled in the center of the gray expanse.

Its voice did not resonate the air to make what we would call sound.

And of course, not a single living being existed within the range of its call.

So there was nothing to hear or understand the Beast's—Chanteur, the First Beast Who Laments for the Moon's—voice.

Still, the Beast continued to howl. A meaningless sound, which would never reach a soul, without fatigue or despair, or even an understanding of those concepts—forever.

By the way, this gray land might all have seemed the same when viewed from above in Regule Aire, but to actually go down onto the surface would surprisingly show how richly the contours of the land had been preserved. Rolling sand dunes where hills once sat. Gray peaks where steep mountains once stood. Ruins that held remnants of what had once been stone buildings standing in place. That was why the salvagers could weave through these remnants, searching for traces of a long-lost civilization.

Now, let us talk about what sat at the feet of the howling Beast.

A small town had stood there a little over five hundred years ago.

It had been neither particularly prosperous, nor did it have any sort of industry for which it was known, but it had a long, respectable history. From the cobbled streets to the trees lining them to the theater to the commuter cart stops to the cheap apartments—they all held a certain dignity, as though embodying a pride from having stood there for centuries.

On the outskirts of town once sat a small orphanage. It had been converted from what was once an ages-old nursery school, so this building, too, had held the air of a long and storied history. In other words, it had been shabby. Whenever it rained, whenever the wind blew, those who'd lived there ran around with boards and hammers.

About three thousand people had lived in the town.

The orphanage had boasted only twenty.

That had been 526 years ago. The scenery of that time now only exists in a certain someone's memory.

And now.

The Beast was howling.

It continued to utter an aimless cry.

Let me spoil something for you.

Once, in the age of the elven elders, it was said members of their community could communicate through their spirits without vibrating the air. What the Beast was doing was very similar to that. A sort of telepathic communication that only those of the same race, of similar mind, could receive.

And each of the Seventeen Beasts were of different races. Chanteur's words could only reach Chanteur.

Chanteur was the only one of its kind. A being so infinitely close to coming to an end in a single body. A search far and wide across the world would never produce anything it could call kin.

That was why there was no destination for this Beast's voice.

No one could hear this Beast's wail.

That was all it has done since first appearing in this world, and the Beast would continue to sing its silent cry.

"———————————D———————a————————d——————————"

The voice of the kinless Beast.
It reached no one. It resonated with no one.
It simply vanished into the gray wasteland.

Afterword/
Or Rather, Behind the Scenes

Greetings, everyone. I'm a new author, Akira Kareno.

I'm sorry. I'm partially kidding. I'm not that new, but this is my first time publishing a book with Sneaker Bunko. I'm glad to meet you through this new series.

For those who start reading from the afterword: The culprit was the master. He did it with an icicle. Just kidding.

The title of this work is *WorldEnd: What Do You Do at the End of the World? Are You Busy? Will You Save Us?* (I'm a little late, but wow, that's long!), but by the end of this first book, no one has really been saved yet. The main character is a bit delicate, so there are no battle-like battles. That's a real spoiler.

In the corner of a dying world, little survivors who wish to live for just a little longer lead desperate, do-or-die, comfortable, lazy, declining lives. Does salvation really exist for them? If it does, what does it look like?

That's the sort of feel I want to evoke with this story, and I hope to put out the second volume soon. As of now, I can't promise anything after that (I am thankful for your support!), but I hope I can go as far as possible.

I had the help of many people while this book was being completed.

ue-san, who gave expression to the faeries through warm illustrations as the schedule picked up speed like a runaway train. Editor G-san, who managed that schedule. My friends, who kept saying, "You need to write sometimes!" The neighborhood cats that soothed my soul in the middle of carnage.

And of course, all of you who are reading this right now.

Thank you so much. I hope you will stick with me.

The next volume is entirely action. A giant intercontinental ballistic robot created by the combination of the double ties of love and hatred mows down a swarm of space monsters. Just kidding.

Summer 2014

AKIRA KARENO